FICTION Harris, Charlaine.
HAR

Sweet and deadly.

$28.95

DATE			

SWEET AND DEADLY

Recent Titles by Charlaine Harris from Severn House

SWEET AND DEADLY
SECRET RAGE

SWEET AND DEADLY

Charlaine Harris

This title published in hardcover format 2010
in Great Britain and in the USA by
SEVERN HOUSE PUBLISHERS LTD of
9–15 High Street, Sutton, Surrey, England, SM1 1DF.
First published in the USA 1981 by Houghton Mifflin
and in mass market by Ballantine in 1985.

British Library Cataloguing in Publication Data

Harris, Charlaine.
  Sweet and deadly.
  1. Traffic accident victims--Fiction. 2. Parents--Death--
  Fiction. 3. Murder--Investigation--Mississippi--Fiction.
  4. Mississippi--Social conditions--Fiction. 5. Suspense
  fiction.
  I. Title II. Harris, Charlaine. Dead dog.
  813.5'4-dc22

  ISBN-13: 978-0-7278-6948-7 (cased)

All Severn House titles are printed on acid-free paper.

Severn House Publishers support The Forest Stewardship Council [FSC],
the leading international forest certification organisation. All our titles that
are printed on Greenpeace-approved FSC-certified paper carry the FSC logo.

 **Mixed Sources**
Product group from well-managed
forests and other controlled sources
www.fsc.org Cert no. SA-COC-1565
© 1996 Forest Stewardship Council

Printed and bound in Great Britain by the
MPG Books Group, Bodmin, Cornwall.

To Hal, who made this possible

1

S HE PASSED A dead dog on her way to the tenant shack.

It was already stiff, the legs poker-straight in rigor. It had been a big dog, maybe dun-colored; with only a quick glimpse, Catherine could not be sure. It was covered in the fine powdery dust that every passing vehicle threw up from the dirt road in the dry Delta summer.

In her rearview mirror she saw the cloud raised by her passage hanging in the air after she had passed, a cloud dividing endless rows of cotton. But the road was too poor to allow many backward glances.

She wondered briefly why someone had been

driving so fast on the caked and rutted dirt that he had not seen the dog in time to swerve.

A sideways look at the cotton told Catherine that it would make a sad crop this year. The heat had lasted too long, unbroken by rain.

This land was Catherine's, had been her great-grandfather's; but Catherine rented it out as her father had done. She was glad she did as she recalled her grandfather's irascibility in bad years, when she had ridden with him across "the place," as cotton planters called their acres.

She didn't remember the heat of those dim summers equaling the ferocity of this one. Even this early in the morning, with dawn not too long past, Catherine was beginning to sweat. Later in the day the glare would be intolerable, without considerable protection, to all but the swarthiest. To someone of Catherine's whiteness of skin it would be disastrous.

She pulled to a stop under an oak, killed the motor and got out. The oak was the only tree to break the stretch of the fields for miles. She stood in its sprawling shadow with her eyes closed, the heat and silence enveloping her. She wrapped herself in them gladly.

The silence came alive. A grasshopper thudded its way across the road from one stand of cotton to the next. A locust rattled at her feet.

She opened her eyes reluctantly and, after reaching into the car for the things she had brought with her, began to walk down the road to the empty tenant shack standing to one side of the intersection of two dirt roads.

The fields were empty of tractors and farm hands. Nothing stirred in the vast brilliant flatness but Catherine.

The sack in her left hand clanked as she walked. The gun in her right hand reflected the sun.

Her mother had raised her to be a lady. Her father had taught her how to shoot.

Catherine laid the gun on a stump in the packed-dirt yard of the tenant house. The bare wood of the house was shiny with age and weathering. A few traces of red paint still clung in the cracks between the planks.

It'll all fall down soon, she thought.

The outhouse behind the shack had collapsed months ago.

Under the spell of the drugging heat and hush, she made an effort to move quietly. The clank of the empty cans was jarring as she pulled them out of the sack and set them in a neat row across the broad stump.

She hardly glanced at the black doorless hole of

the shack's entrance. She did notice that the sagging porch seemed even closer to deserting the rest of the house than it had the last time she had driven out of town to shoot.

The dust plumed under her feet as she paced away from the stump. She counted under her breath.

A trickle of sweat started down the nape of her neck, and she was irritated that she had forgotten to bring an elastic band to lift the black hair off her shoulders.

The twinge of irritation faded as she turned to face the stump. Her head bowed. She concentrated on her body's memory of the gun.

In one motion, her head snapped back, her knees bent slightly, her left hand swung up to grip her rising right forearm, and she fired.

A can flew up in the air, landing with a hollow jangle under the steps rising to the porch. Then another. And another.

By the time only one can was left, Catherine was mildly pleased with herself. She dampened her self-congratulations with the reflection that she was, after all, firing from short range. But then, a .32 was not meant for distance shooting.

The last can proved stubborn. Catherine emptied the remaining bullets from the gun at it. She cursed mildly under her breath when the can remained obstinately unpunctured and upright.

It's a good time for a break, she decided.

She trudged back to the stump and collapsed, with her back against its roughness. Pulling a plastic bullet box from a pocket in her blue jeans, she set it on the ground beside her. She eased the pin from the chamber, letting it fall into her hand. She reloaded lazily, full of the languorous peace that follows catharsis.

When the gun was ready, she didn't feel like rising.

Let the can sit, she thought. It deserves to stay on the stump.

She was enjoying the rare moment of relaxation. She laced her fingers across her stomach and noticed that they were leaving smudges on her white T-shirt. Her jeans were coated with dust now. She slapped her thigh lightly and watched the motes fly up.

I'll go home, she thought comfortably, and pop every stitch I have on into the washer. And I'll take a long, long shower. And then—

There was no "then."

But I'm better, she continued, smoothly gliding over the faint uneasiness that had ruffled her peace. I'm better now.

A horsefly landed on her arm, and she slapped at it

automatically. It buzzed away in pique, only to be replaced in short order by one of its companions.

"Damn flies," she muttered.

There sure are a lot of them, she thought in some surprise, as another landed on her knee. Attracted by my sweat, I guess.

That settled it. She would gather up the cans and go back to Lowfield, back to her cool quiet house.

Catherine rose and walked toward the dilapidated porch briskly, slapping at her arms as she went.

The flies were whirring in and out of the open doorway, creating a drone in the stillness. The boarded-up windows of the house and the overhanging roof of its porch combined to make a dark cave of the interior. The sun penetrated only a foot into the entrance, so the darkness seemed impenetrable by contrast.

She stooped to pick up the first can she had hit, which was lodged under the lopsided steps. The stoop leveled her with the raised floor of the house, built high to avoid flooding in the heavy Delta rains. As she reached for the punctured can, something caught at the corner of her eye, an image so odd that she froze, doubled over, her hand extended for the can.

There was something in that little pool of light penetrating the empty doorway.

It was a hand.

She tried to identify it as something else, anything else.

It remained a hand. The palm was turned up, and the fingers stretched toward Catherine appealingly. Catherine's eyes flicked down to her own extended fingers, then back. She straightened very slowly.

When she inhaled, she realized she had been holding her breath against the smell. It was a whiff of the same odor she had caught as her car passed the dead dog.

With no thought at all, she grasped one of the supports that held up the roof over the porch. Moving quietly and carefully, she pulled herself up on the loose rotting planks and took a little step forward.

A fly buzzed past her face.

The blinding contrast of sun and gloom lessened as she crept closer. When she reached the doorway she could see what lay inside the shack.

The hand was still attached to a wrist, the wrist to an arm . . .

It had been a woman.

Her face was turned away from Catherine. Even in the dimness, Catherine could make out dark patches matting the gray hair. She realized then what made the head so oddly shaped.

A fly landed on the woman's arm.

Catherine began shaking. She was afraid her knees would give way, that she would fall on top of the stinking thing. Her stomach began to twist.

She backed away, tiny shuffling steps that took all her concentration. Her arm touched a wooden support. She had reached the edge of the porch.

She turned to grip the support, then lowered a foot until it rested firmly on the ground.

She reached the stump and sat on its uneven surface, with her back to the tenant house. She stared across her land.

"Oh my God," she whispered.

And the fear hit her. After a stunned second she scrabbled in the dust for her gun.

Her eyes darted around her, searching.

Nothing moved on the road, or in the fields; but she felt terrifyingly exposed in that vast flatness.

The car. She had to make it to the car. It was only a few yards away, parked under the oak's inadequate shade. All she had to do was cross those yards. But she was frozen in position like an animal caught in headlights.

The sheriff, she thought with sudden clarity. I've got to get Sheriff Galton.

With that thought, that plain plan, she was able to launch herself from the stump.

She opened the door and shoved the pistol to the other side of the car with shaking fingers, then slid into the driver's seat. Shut the door. Locked it. She managed to turn the key in the ignition before her muscles refused to obey her. Her fingers on the gearshift were too palsied to put the car into drive.

She screamed at her helplessness. She covered her ears against the ragged sound.

But with that release, her shaking lessened. She could put the car in gear and start back home to Lowfield.

2

THERE WERE TWO houses where the dirt road joined the highway. Catherine could have stopped at either and found help.

She never thought of it. In a fog of shock she had fixed her destination, and she would not stop until she reached it. She drove south on the highway without seeing anything but the concrete in front of her.

To reach the sheriff's office, she had to turn off the highway into the town. When she saw the familiar brick building sitting squarely in front of the old jail, Catherine felt dizzy with relief.

The lights inside the little building were on. Through the glass door Catherine could see the dispatcher, Mary Jane Cory, seated at her desk behind the counter.

It took an immense effort of will to unclamp her hands from the wheel, open the car door, swing her legs out, and force the rest of her body to follow them.

"Good morning, Catherine! I'll be with you in a minute," Mrs. Cory said briskly, and thudded out a few more words on her ancient typewriter.

In what later seemed to Catherine insanity, she kept silent and waited obediently. She leaned on the counter, her hands gripping the far edge of it to keep upright.

That silence alerted some warning signal in Mary Jane Cory. She gave Catherine a second glance and then was on her feet, her hands covering Catherine's.

"What's the matter?" the older woman asked sharply.

"The sheriff . . . I want to see the sheriff," Catherine said painfully. Her jaws ached from long clenching.

"Are you going to faint, Catherine?" Mrs. Cory asked, still in that sharp watchful voice.

Catherine didn't answer.

Mrs. Cory switched her grip from Catherine's hands to her upper arms and called without turning her head, "James Galton! Come here quick!"

There was a stir in the office that had "Sheriff" on the door. The roar of the air conditioning covered the sound of Galton's quiet steps, but a khaki-covered elbow appeared in Catherine's range of view, propped on the counter beside her.

"You got troubles, Catherine?" rumbled a carefully relaxed voice. Catherine saw Mrs. Cory's platinum head give a shake in answer to some silent query of Galton's.

Now that the time had come to deliver her message, Catherine found herself curiously embarrassed, as if she were about to commit a deliberate faux pas.

She turned her head stiffly to look up at Galton.

"There's a dead woman in an old tenant house. On the place."

"You sure she's dead?"

Catherine's face was blank as she stared at him. "Oh, yes," she said.

"A black woman?"

"No," she said, and felt the ripple of surprise. Lowfield white women did not get themselves dumped in tenant shacks.

"Do you know who it is?"

"No. No." Her voice sounded odd to her own ears. "She's covered in blood."

Galton's face changed as she stared at him. He didn't look like the relaxed and genial Jimmy Galton who had been her father's friend.

He looked like the sheriff.

⁂

Catherine had assumed she could go home after informing the sheriff of her discovery.

She had, she soon realized, been thinking like a child.

Galton issued a few commands to Mrs. Cory, who got busy on the radio and telephone. He gently but quite firmly led Catherine into his office, guided her to the chair in front of his desk, and then eased himself into his own battered chair.

"You want to go to the doctor for a tranquilizer?"

But the doctor was her father. He was dead.

No, she thought, horrified. No. She shook her head to clear her thoughts. This kind of confusion hadn't happened to her in a long time; she had thought it was over with.

"Want something to drink?"

"No," she whispered.

He indicated his pack of cigarettes.

Catherine forced herself to reach for one and light it, while Galton eyed her intently.

He's trying to see if I can do it by myself, Catherine thought suddenly. Her back stiffened.

"Now, I'm going to ask you a few questions. You just take your time answering," he said.

Catherine nodded briefly.

He was being kind in a stern way, but Catherine realized that the day would be longer than she had ever imagined when she arose early that morning to go target shooting.

Galton jogged her with a couple of questions. Once she got going, she gave a clear account of her morning.

There was nothing much to tell.

When she finished, Galton rose without a word, patting her absently as he passed into the outer room.

Catherine heard a shuffling of feet in the main office, a murmur of voices. Mrs. Cory had called in the deputies.

Catherine looked down at her hands clenched in her lap. Her heavy dark hair swung forward, shielding her face, giving her a tiny corner of privacy against the open door.

The look of her twined fingers, the smell of the sheriff's office, and the scrape of official boots had ripped the cover from a well of memory. For a few moments she was not in Lowfield but in a similar police station in a similar tiny town, in Arkansas. She was not wearing blue jeans but the dress she had worn to work that day. Her parents had been dead for four hours instead of six months.

With a terrible effort, she wrenched herself back into her proper place.

I will not give way, she told herself ferociously. I will get through this and I will not give way.

She listened to Sheriff Galton's voice rumbling in the main office. He was telling Mary Jane Cory to call enough men for a coroner's jury.

<hr/>

She rode back to the shack in the sheriff's car. The car was bright green with gold lettering and a star on the side. She could see people glancing in as the sheriff drove past, then looking again as they identified Galton's passenger as Catherine Linton.

Though she had cut herself off from the mainstream of life in Lowfield, Catherine was fully aware that the talk would already be beginning. A month ago, it would not have occurred to her to care.

"Catherine," Galton said.

She looked at him.

"Who rents your place?"

"Martin Barnes," she said promptly.

She slid easily back into her silence. It had been her natural element for months; and even before that, she had not been what anyone would call talkative. Her roommate in college had called her "Sphinx." It had become her accepted name on the small private campus.

She wished there was someone around to call her that now.

Martin Barnes. That was food for thought. Catherine supposed the person most familiar with that piece of land must be the most suspected. The shack was visible, but not obvious, from the highway. You wouldn't, Catherine decided, just glimpse it and say, "Perfect place for this body I have on my hands." But Mr. Barnes can't have anything to do with this, she thought. He's—older than my father; he's a good man. Besides—she must have been raped. Why else would anyone drag a lady out to the country and bash her on the head?

But the woman's dress hadn't been disarranged. Catherine could see it clearly, pulled down around the woman's knees. A print shirtwaist dress, an everyday dress, short-sleeved for the summer. The kind of dress any older woman in Lowfield would wear to go to the grocery. Not a dress any woman would wear to die in.

Robbery, then? Catherine wondered. Had there

been a purse at the woman's side? She couldn't recall one—and she could still see the body clearly. She shuddered, and her small square hands gripped her folded arms.

"Let me tell you the procedure, Catherine," Sheriff Galton said abruptly, and she knew he had noticed the shudder.

She summoned up a courteous show of interest.

"First we secure the scene."

The thought of anyone "securing" the ramshackle tenant house made her want to laugh, but she pressed her lips together and locked in the urge. Everyone thinks you're crazy anyway: don't confirm it, she warned herself. She inclined her head to show that she was listening.

"Percy here will take some pictures," Galton proceeded with a matter-of-fact air.

Percy was the black deputy lodged in the back seat with a lot of camera paraphernalia. He was a solemn-faced young man, and as Catherine turned to look at him by way of acknowledging his entrance into the conversation, she felt an unexpected stir of recognition. Before she could place it, Galton rumbled on.

"Mary Jane's called the coroner, and he'll convene a coroner's jury at the scene. They'll hear your testimony and they'll give their finding."

Then I can go home, Catherine thought hopefully.

"Then you come back to the station, make a formal statement, sign it."

Damn.

"Then you can go home. I may have to ask you a few more questions later, but I think that'll be it. Until we catch the perpetrator. Then there'll be the trial."

Trial opened up new vistas of trouble. It sounded pretty cocky on James Galton's part, too.

Catherine glanced at Galton's stern lined face, and suddenly she decided it would be a mistake to underestimate Sheriff James Galton.

The sheriff's car and the deputies' car following it turned off the highway onto the dirt road Catherine indicated. The sun was higher, the glare brighter than during Catherine's early morning venture. She had no sunglasses and had to lower the visor to shield her eyes. She was too short for it to help much.

"This your grandfather's place?" Galton asked.

"All of it."

"All rented out to Martin?"

"Yes. For years. Daddy rented to him too."

Catherine lit a cigarette from the battered pack in her pocket and smoked it slowly.

The shack at the crossroads came into view.

The weathered wood shone in the sun. It looked so quiet and empty that for a brief moment Catherine doubted what she had seen. Then she began shaking again, and dug her nails into her arms to keep from crying.

I'm not going in there. Surely they won't ask me to go in there, she thought.

"This the place?" Galton asked.

She nodded.

They pulled to a halt under the same oak that had sheltered Catherine's car. The sheriff and the deputy got out immediately. Catherine put out her cigarette with elaborate care. The black deputy opened her door.

She left the sheriff's car and began to walk down the road.

The sweat that had dried in the sheriff's cold office had formed a layer on her skin. Now she sweated again. She felt filthy and old.

She ignored Galton, the black deputy, and the other deputies from the second car. The dark emptiness of the doorway grew with every step she took. She imagined she could hear the drone of the flies already.

It was not just her imagination that she could

pick up the smell when she reached the stump. She stopped in her tracks. The rising temperature and the passage of even this short amount of time had done their work.

She would not go farther.

"In there," she said briefly.

The sheriff had picked up the scent for himself. Catherine watched his mouth set grimly. She got some satisfaction from that, though she was ashamed of it.

The other deputies had caught up. In a knot, the brown uniforms approached the cabin slowly.

She could see the full force of the smell hit them. A wavering of heads, a look of disgust.

"Jesus!" one of them muttered.

The sheriff was eyeing the rickety porch with calculation. Catherine weighed about 115 pounds; the sheriff close to 185.

With a kind of detached interest, Catherine wondered how he would manage.

Galton scanned his deputies from the neck down, and picked Ralph Carson, who had gone to high school with Catherine, as the lightest of the group.

After some muttered consultation, Carson edged up on the porch, gingerly picked his way across, and reached the door frame without the porch collapsing.

He looked in. When he turned to extend an arm to the sheriff, his face was set in harsh lines of control, and his tan looked muddy.

Galton gripped Carson's arm, and the deputy gave a heave inward. After Galton, the black deputy was hoisted into the shack. The others began to search the barren area around the house.

I guess I thought it would be gone by the time we got here, Catherine thought with a mixture of relief and dismay. Her tension drained away suddenly, leaving her sick and exhausted. She sat down on the stump, her back turned to the open doorway, which was now occasionally lit with the quick glare of flash bulbs.

A white and orange ambulance was bumping its way down the road. A deputy flagged it in behind the official cars, and two white-coated attendants and Dr. Jerry Selforth, Lowfield's new doctor, jumped out. After exchanging a few words with the deputy, Selforth detached himself from the little group and came toward Catherine.

"Good morning, Jerry," Catherine said with polite incongruity. He's excited by this, she thought.

"Hey, Catherine, you all right?" He massaged her shoulder. He couldn't talk to a woman without prodding, rubbing, gripping. Men he slapped on the back.

She was too tired to pull away, but her eyebrows rose in a frigid arch. Jerry's hand dropped away.

"I'm sorry you had to find her like that," he said more soberly.

Catherine shrugged.

"Well . . ." the young doctor murmured after a beat of silence.

Catherine whipped herself into more courtesy.

"Your first?" she inquired, tilting her head toward the shack.

"My first that's been dead longer than two hours," he admitted. "Since med school. There's a pathologist in Morene that'll come help me."

"They were better preserved in med school," he added thoughtfully, as a short-lived breeze wafted east.

"Dr. Selforth!" bellowed Galton from the interior of the cabin.

Jerry flashed Catherine a broad grin and trotted cheerfully away.

He certainly fit right into his slot in Lowfield, Catherine thought wryly. She had heard the ladies loved him, and after a residence of five months, he was first-naming everyone in town.

Catherine had not liked Jerry Selforth, who had taken over her father's practice almost lock, stock, and barrel, since the time he had laughed at her father's old-fashioned office in back of the Linton home. To her further irritation, Jerry Selforth had been much smitten with her black hair and white skin, and he had lengthened the business of purchasing Dr. Linton's office equipment considerably, apparently in the hope of arousing a similar enthusiasm in Catherine.

Because of the dates she had refused, she always felt she had an obligation to be kind to him, though it was an uphill effort. Something about Jerry Selforth's smile said outright that his bed was a palace of delights that Catherine would be lucky to share.

Catherine had her doubts about that.

Time limped by, and the stump grew uncomfortable. Rivulets of sweat trickled down her face. Her skin prickled ominously, a prelude to sunburn. She wondered what she was doing there. She was clearly redundant.

She had felt the same way when other people, to spare her, had made all the arrangements about her parents' bodies. The sheriff in Parkinson, Arkansas, had been shorter, heavyset. He had been kind, too. She had accepted a tranquilizer that day. After it entered her blood stream, she had been able to call her boss at her first job, to tell him she wouldn't be coming back.

A flurry of dust announced new arrivals. Catherine

was glad to have something new to look at, to break her painful train of thought. Three more cars pulled up behind the ambulance. The lead car was a white Lincoln Continental that was certainly going to need a wash after this morning was over.

As the driver emerged, Catherine recognized him. It was her neighbor, Carl Perkins. He and his wife lived in an incredible pseudoantebellum structure across the street from the west side of Catherine's own house. Its construction had had the whole town agape for months.

Catherine suddenly felt like laughing as she recalled Tom Mascalco's first comment on that house. Whenever he drove by, Tom said, he expected a chorus of darkies to appear on the veranda and hum "Tara's Theme."

Catherine's flash of humor faded when she remembered that Carl Perkins was, in addition to his many other irons in the town fire, the county coroner. The men piling out of the other cars must comprise the coroner's jury, she realized. She knew them all: local businessmen, planters. There was one black— Cleophus Hames, who ran one of the two Negro funeral parlors.

I wish I was invisible, she thought miserably.

She became very still and looked down the short length of her legs at her tennis shoes.

Of course, if I don't look at them, they can't see me, she jeered at herself, when she realized what she was doing.

But it worked for a while. The men stood in an uneasy bunch several feet from the shack, not talking much, just glancing at the doorway with varying degrees of apprehension.

It worked until Sheriff Galton drew all eyes to her by jumping from the cabin doorway and striding directly to Catherine's stump.

She had surreptitiously raised the hem of her T-shirt to wipe some of the sweat from her face, so she didn't observe the set of his shoulders until it was too late to be alerted. She had a bare second to realize something was wrong.

"Why did you say you didn't know her?" he asked brusquely when he was within hearing distance.

"What?" she said stupidly.

She couldn't understand what he meant. The heat and the long wait had drained her. Her brain stirred sluggishly under the sting of his voice.

Galton stood in front of her now, no longer familiar and sympathetic but somehow menacing.

He said angrily, "You've known that woman all your life."

⁂

She stared up at him until the sun dazzled her eyes unbearably and she had to raise an arm to shield them.

The cold stirring deep inside her was fear, fear that activated a store of self-defense she had never been called upon to use.

"I never saw her face. I told you that," she said. Her pale gray eyes held his with fierce intensity. "The side of her head nearest me was covered with blood." Her voice was sharp, definite. For the first time in her life she was speaking to an older person, a lifelong acquaintance, in a tone that was within a stone's throw of rudeness.

She saw in his face that he had not missed it.

"You better think again, Catherine," he retorted. "That's Leona Gaites, who was your father's nurse for thirty-odd years."

C ATHERINE GAPED AT him.

"What on earth . . ." she stammered. "Miss Gaites . . . what is she doing out here?"

Even through her shock Catherine saw some relief touch Galton's face. Her unalloyed amazement must have gone some way toward convincing him of her ignorance of the dead woman's identity. Her innocence.

My innocence? Her anger grew. It felt surprisingly good. She was so seldom overtly angry.

"Well, come on," Galton was saying in a more relaxed voice. "The coroner's jury is here. You have to testify."

Catherine lost that portion of the day. While she automatically delivered her simple account to a ring of sober faces, she was remembering Miss Gaites.

The incongruity of seeing starched, immaculate Leona Gaites in such a state!

She must have given me a hundred suckers, Catherine thought, her childhood crowding around her.

The suckers had been a bribe to convince Catherine that Leona liked her.

It hadn't worked. Leona hadn't liked children at all.

So Catherine had disliked Miss Gaites, had not even accorded her the courtesy of "Miss Leona." She had disliked the way the starched uniform rattled when the tall woman walked, had disliked the hair that seemed set upon Miss Gaites's head instead of growing there.

Most of all, Catherine had disliked the pity she was obliged to feel for Miss Gaites, who had no family.

Her father had always praised his nurse highly to his wife and daughter, insisting with overdone joviality that Leona kept his office together. The forced note in his insistence told Catherine that even her amiable father could not find it in him to wholeheartedly like Leona Gaites.

Catherine remembered the tears sliding down Leona's square handsome face at the double funeral.

She shouldn't have died like that, Catherine thought, as she watched the coroner's jury being heaved across the porch and into the shack. A dog shouldn't die like that. Then Catherine remembered the dog's corpse she had passed that morning. The same person killed them both, she thought with surprising certainty. Driving too fast, to get away from what he did to Miss Gaites.

⁂

The coroner's jury viewed the body and came to the obvious conclusion. Murder, they found.

Catherine cast a last look at the covered figure, now bundled onto a stretcher borne by the two sweat-soaked cursing attendants, on its way to Jerry Self-orth's eager knife.

As she watched the load sliding into the back of the ambulance, she saw one of the attendants gag from the smell.

Leona had always been so clean.

Catherine began to walk down the baked dirt road toward the sheriff's car. The coroner, Carl Perkins, fell into step beside her.

She looked at him with new eyes. Familiar people

were no longer familiar. The anger and suspicion in Sheriff Galton's face had shaken her out of taking for granted people she had known since childhood.

"Terrible thing," Perkins muttered. He was obviously upset. His big hands were shoved into the pockets of his working khakis.

He must have been gardening when Mrs. Cory phoned him, Catherine thought dully. She watched Carl and Molly Perkins working in their yard every weekend, provided she herself had remembered to have her hedge trimmed.

"Yes," Catherine replied belatedly.

"I'm sorry for you, that you had to find her."

There was real regret in his voice, and Catherine warmed to him. "If I hadn't happened to shoot cans this morning—" she began, and stopped.

Perkins wrinkled his forehead inquiringly.

His eyebrows are too sparse to count, Catherine noticed. He's really getting old.

She spoke hastily to cover her stare. "She wouldn't have been found for a long time, if no one had worked in those fields until—" "Until the smell was gone," she meant to say, but couldn't.

"You're right," he said. He was angry: his voice sounded hoarse and strained. "Wonder if Galton can handle this? All he's used to are Saturday night cut-tings."

They had reached the sheriff's car, where Galton was directing two deputies to stay behind and continue to search.

"Now, you come over and see us," Perkins said earnestly. "You've been a stranger since your folks have been gone."

Yes, she thought. I've been a stranger.

"Is all your father's business tended to?" he asked into the blank wall of her silence.

"Yes," Catherine replied, shaking herself. She would have to say more, she realized after a second. "Jerry Selforth bought almost all Dad's equipment. We were lucky to get another doctor in town so soon. Dr. Anderson's so old that I know having Jerry take the practice is a relief to him."

"It was a surprise," said Mr. Perkins. "Not too many young men want to come to Lowfield."

His bleak tone made Catherine raise her eyebrows. She didn't like Jerry Selforth much as a man, but the town had desperately needed him as a doctor. What had Jerry done to offend her neighbor?

Just then the ambulance started up, and the people by the cars had to step between them to let it edge by.

Catherine's thoughts flew back to Leona Gaites,

and she scarcely noticed Carl Perkin's farewell nod as he went down the road to his Lincoln, in the wake of the ambulance.

The narrow dirt road became busy with flying dust and confusion as the accumulated vehicles reversed to point back to the highway. The cars formed a train like a funeral procession behind the hearse of the orange and white ambulance.

<hr />

The black deputy was detailed to take Catherine's statement.

"Then head on over to Leona Gaites's house," Sheriff Galton added when he was halfway out the door. "Bring the camera."

The young black man nodded briskly and turned to Catherine, who was huddled in a corner hoping she was out of the way.

"Miss Catherine, would you come over here, please?" he said, indicating a straight-backed chair by a scarred desk.

Catherine could tell from the set of Mary Jane Cory's back that she disapproved of this black policeman. The unnatural brightness of Mrs. Cory's voice as she spoke to him contrasted sharply with the natural tone in which she spoke to a couple of blacks who entered the station as supplicants.

Catherine was beyond caring who took down her statement; but she was less comfortable with blacks in her own town than she was with blacks anywhere else. Upon taking up her life in Lowfield after her parents' death, she had found sadly that the old attitudes caught at her and strangled her attempts to be easy in an uneasy situation.

The deputy's name tag read "Eakins," Catherine noticed for the first time. Now she could place the familiarity of the man's face.

"Your mother is Betty, isn't she?" Catherine asked, as he rolled typing paper into the machine.

"Yes, Ma'am," he said reluctantly, and Catherine felt a pit-of-the-stomach dismay.

Betty Eakins had been the Lintons' maid for years, until she had grown too old and arthritic to work any more.

Catherine had never called their maid anything but "Betty"; and she had decided, after a year away in college, that that was a shameful thing. Catherine had not even known Betty's last name for the first years of the woman's employment. Catherine's visits home had been more and more awkward as her awareness of what lay around her became acute, to the point that Catherine was secretly glad when Betty grew too infirm to iron the Lintons' sheets. Catherine's parents had died before they could replace Betty with another maid.

"How is she?" asked Catherine. She had to say something, she felt.

"Mama's fine," he said curtly. Percy Eakins's face rivaled Catherine's for blankness.

"She's a very old woman now," he said more gently—whether out of fear of being rude to a white woman or because he sensed Catherine's misery, she couldn't tell. She chose to regard his softened tone as absolution for the sin of having offended racially.

"I'll tell her I saw you. She talks about you all the time," he said finally.

And their personal conversation was closed.

He took her statement in a meticulous professional manner, in question-and-answer form.

"Your full name?"

"Catherine Scott Linton."

"Your age?"

"Twenty-three."

"Place of employment and position?"

"The *Lowfield Gazette*. I'm the society editor."

"Your present place of residence?"

"Corner of Mayhew and Linton."

No one in Lowfield had ever felt a need for house numbers. The street her house faced had been named for her great-grandfather, when the town was bustling and the river was close. Now the river was two miles away, held in check by the levee, and Lowfield's population had not fluctuated appreciably in her father's lifetime.

"On the morning of July 11, what did you do?"

"I went out to some land I own, north of Lowfield."

"For what purpose?"

"To practice target shooting . . ."

S HE CAME IN the side door from the garage. Her
coffee cup and the empty percolator still stood on
the counter, waiting to be washed. The hands of the
kitchen clock glided electrically smooth on their
course.

She was almost surprised that the house was the
same, so much had passed since she had left it that
morning.

She stood in the middle of the bright tiled floor
and listened. She had never done that before.

Catherine shook herself when she realized what
she was doing, and started down the long hallway
that divided the house, beginning at the kitchen and
ending at a bathroom.

But she looked quickly into each doorway as she passed. She saw only the big familiar lifeless rooms, lovingly (and lavishly) redecorated by her mother. She paused in the doorway of the formal living room, where her parents had entertained, and suddenly recalled her father half-ruefully telling guests, "Rachel's rebuilt this old house from the inside out." It was the only room Catherine had changed.

At the end of the hall Catherine almost went right into her old bedroom. It's been months since I did that, she thought.

She went straight through the master bedroom to its cool tiled bathroom and shed everything she had on. She stepped into the shower, but not before self-consciously locking the bathroom door.

She had never done that before, either.

The shower was bliss. With cool water shooting over her, washing off the layers of dust and sweat, she was able to forget the shack for a few minutes.

She dried herself and combed out her wet hair slowly. She lay down on the big bed and hoped for sleep, but her body hummed with tension like a telephone line. Finally she quit hoping and got up, padding across the heavy carpeting to the closet and folding back a mirrored door to pull out a long loose lounging dress, pale gray and scattered with red poppies. She yanked it over her head and went down the hall to the kitchen, where she began searching the refrigerator.

Good. Beer. With one of those in me, I bet I can sleep. I'm glad Tom left some.

Armed with the beer and a fresh pack of cigarettes, Catherine wandered into the living room. She settled in her favorite chair, which she had pulled out of its original spot so she could look out the bay window. She had arranged beside it a heavy round table, and, some time later, another chair to keep the first one company. It was her own little base in a house too big for one person; a house still echoing with loss.

The old home across the street had been renovated into the town library. It closed at eleven on Saturday, so Catherine was just in time to see Mrs. Weilenmann, the librarian, lock the front door. Mrs. Weilenmann was the town wonder: an educated northern black woman, who spoke with no trace of the heavy accent white Southerners associated with blacks. And, rumor had it, Mrs. Weilenmann, a widow, had acquired her name by marrying a white man. It was a bandage to Catherine's conscience that Mrs. Weilenmann had gotten the librarian's job. The only wonder, as Catherine saw it, was that she wanted it.

I meant to go to the library today when I got back, Catherine recalled, glancing down at the heap of books on the floor as Mrs. Weilenmann maneuvered her Toyota out of the library parking lot.

Catherine reckoned she had enough to read to last until Monday. And took a swallow of beer to celebrate that minor goodness.

A possible diversion occurred to her. She craned forward to see if Mr. Drummond next door was holding true to form in his late-Saturday-morning grass mowing. But the lawn beyond the hedge that bordered Catherine's yard was empty. She was disappointed and puzzled. She faithfully witnessed Mr. Drummond's ritual each summer Saturday. After a moment, she remembered that the Drummonds were still in Europe, and shook her head at her forgetfulness.

Perhaps she could move her chair to face a side window. She could look across Mayhew Street, see if the Perkinses were back at work in their yard.

It didn't seem worth the trouble.

I'll just sit and drink my beer, she decided. Maybe I'll think of something to do to use up this blasted day.

Her eyes fell on a half-finished book. She considered reading, but decided she couldn't concentrate enough. The book was a murder mystery. Not such a good thing to read today. Her mouth twisted wryly.

After a moment Catherine wriggled deeper into the big chair, stretching her legs to rest them on its matching ottoman. She drank some more beer. She was profoundly bored, yet very tense. She decided it was a horrible combination.

"Toes, relax," she said out loud, suddenly recalling an acting-class exercise. "Feet, relax."

She had worked up to her pelvis when she was diverted by a car pulling onto the graveled apron at the end of the walkway in front of the house. She suspended her exercise in astonishment.

The car was familiar, but she couldn't place the owner. Not Tom, her only occasional visitor. He would merely stroll across to her back door from his own.

"It's Randall Gerrard!" she muttered. Her employer had never come to see her before.

She didn't realize the impact the beer had had on her empty stomach until she got up.

Instead of straightening up the pile of books, instead of fluffling out her damp hair, Catherine stared at Randall as he came up the walkway.

She itemized his heavy shoulders and thick chest, surprising on a man of his height. Especially surprising on a man who had, Catherine told herself, no butt at all.

The sun glinted on the thick reddish-brown hair of his head and beard, and winked off his heavy glasses.

How old must he be now? she wondered. Thirty-five?

She stood riveted and staring. Like a fool, she told herself when she finally roused. She had just begun to move when he knocked on the door, and she could only be grateful he had not glanced at the window.

"Please come in," she said. The beer soaked her voice with a duchesslike formality. She blinked in surprise.

Randall's face, which had been grave, lit with amusement. She followed his glance down to her hand that had gestured him in with a gracious flourish. She saw, appalled, that she was still clutching the beer can. Her elaborate sweep had slopped beer all over her hand.

"Oh *damn*!" she muttered.

He said gently, "Catherine."

To her horror, that note of kindness tipped her into collapse. She began to cry. She twisted away to hide her face, covered her mouth to muffle the ugly sound. She hated for anyone to see her crumple.

A heavy arm went around her, and she instantly twitched away. But she didn't move when the arm firmly encircled her again.

She was somehow deposited on a convenient couch. She dimly heard footsteps crossing the floor and going purposefully down the hall. She looked up as Randall reappeared with a box of tissues. She blessed him mentally, and lowered her face. She was acutely aware of how dreadful she looked when she cried. As she cleaned her face, she felt the tears dry up inside her.

Catherine waited until she could hope that her nose had returned to its normal color before she brushed her hair back and looked sideways at him . . . and surprised something in Randall's face that amazed her, something unmistakable; though it had been a long time since she had cared to recognize it in a man's face.

Empty and giddy, Catherine felt a pleasant little jolt of lust. She had seen and thought too much of death to deny that positive celebration of life.

"Better?" Randall asked, with a fair assumption of gravity.

"Yes, thank you," she answered with dignity.

He handed her the beer can. Catherine took a size-able swallow. Her eyes were on his face—a Slavic peasant face, she thought darkly—as he looked around the room, zeroed in on her arrangement in the bay window. The soft chair with the dent her body had left, the paperback with a bookmark thrust inside, the lamp pulled over close to her chair surrounded by a litter of books: it looked like what it was, the habitual den of a solitary person. From where she was sitting now, Catherine thought, it looked pitiful.

"If you heard so fast," she said hastily, "then . . ."

An impatient knock on the back door finished her sentence.

"Tom," Catherine said simply.

She was regretting the end of a promising moment as she went through the den at the rear of the house to answer the knock.

⁂

As she had predicted, it was Tom, her only full-time fellow reporter. His long lean frame bisected the doorway.

"Are you all right" he asked perfunctorily. His mouth had already opened to begin firing questions when Catherine cut him short.

"You might as well come on in the living room, Randall's in there," she said.

Tom looked almost comically taken aback.

Catherine, bowled over by giddiness, nearly laughed as she preceded Tom into the living room.

"Hey, Randall," he said casually, folding his length into an uncomfortable Victorian rosewood chair. Then he forgot to be offhand. "The coroner's jury said murder, of course. And a *Gazette* reporter found the body! Jesus, what a story!" He yanked his fearsome Fu Manchu mustache so fiercely that Catherine thought he might pull the hair out.

"Calm down, Tom, it's not like there was another paper to scoop," Randall said. He took his pipe from his pocket.

"Hey Catherine, is there any of that beer left?" Tom asked, sidetracked into showing Randall that he, Tom, had been there first.

"Three or four," Catherine said. "Randall, would you care for a beer?"

Randall accepted.

It seemed to Catherine that she took forever pulling out the tabs on three cans, pouring them, and putting the glasses on a tray.

Pouring them out seemed an unnecessary refinement, but she was determined to do everything right.

When Catherine came in with the beer, Randall and Tom were discussing rearrangement of the front page to handle the murder story. The paper only came out on Wednesdays, so there was plenty of time to think about it.

After she had handed the glasses around and resumed her seat, she realized the men were eyeing her with longing—for her story. Randall Gerrard and Tom Mascalco had print in their blood—the only thing they had in common, Catherine thought.

Randall had inherited the *Gazette* when his elder brother, for whom it had been intended, had shaken that dust of Lowfield off his shoes and headed for the fertile fields of Atlanta. In fact, Randall had abandoned a promising career doing something in Washington (Catherine couldn't remember exactly what), to come home when his father died.

However deep Randall's regret over that lost career might be, his raising had implanted in him enough of the newsman's passion for a story, and enough love for the Delta, to bend his will toward building up the *Gazette*.

Tom had worked for Randall for three months. He was younger than Catherine. The recent glut of journalism majors had made him glad to accept a job, even at the *Gazette*.

Tom was possessed, Catherine had observed, by a Woodward-and-Bernstein complex, which had led to some interesting clashes with Randall. Tom was restless with hunger for big stories, scandals. Catherine sometimes felt she had a tiger in her backyard since she had rented Tom her father's old office to live in.

"I'm all right, if you want to ask questions," she said with a sigh. After all, she thought, I'm a newspaper person myself. In a rinky-dink kind of way.

"You sure?" Randall had the grace to ask.

"Yes."

Catherine knew that Tom had only been held in check by Randall's presence. His pad and pencil had been ready in his hand when he knocked on the door.

In a clear monotone, she went through her story again. She wished it were more exciting, since she had had to tell it so often.

"Galton. Jerry Selforth," Tom mumbled when she had finished, scribbling a list of people he wanted to interview.

"Who were her friends, Catherine?" he asked, pencil poised to write.

He looked up impatiently when she didn't reply.

"I don't know," she said slowly, surprised. "I don't think Miss Gaites *had* friends. She didn't go to church or to the bridge club, or anything like that. She told my father she saw enough people at the office every day to make her sick of them."

And Catherine had to admit at that moment that her own attitude was much the same.

The thought of becoming a Leona Gaites frightened her.

"When was the last time you saw Leona?" Randall asked in his slow voice.

"When she helped me go through the things left in Father's office; things Jerry Selforth didn't want to buy. They had to be moved out of the house before Tom moved in. We put them up in the attic over there. Some old filing cabinets. I think a few other things."

"Not since then?" Tom asked. "I thought you had known her for years."

"Yes, I have—had. But that doesn't mean I liked her."

The two men seemed startled by this statement, which Catherine had delivered with bland finality. She returned their look impassively. They had not expected this from her, she saw. She really must have presented a skimmed-milk image.

"Have you talked to Jerry Selforth, Tom?" Randall asked.

"Just for a second. He hasn't done the autopsy. The pathologist in Morene won't get here till late this afternoon. From a preliminary examination, he doesn't think she was raped. She wasn't killed at the shack, either. She was already dead when she was dumped there. He thinks she'd been dead since early last night."

"*Why?*" Randall asked himself.

Catherine's head swung up. She stared at him blindly.

A reason formed in her head. It caused her such pain that she couldn't recognize it for a moment. Something thumped and shuddered inside her. An enormous wound, compounded of deep grief and un-released anger, just beginning to heal, broke open afresh.

"Did she have money?" Tom was asking. He sounded far away.

"Oh no," Randall said. "If she had, she kept it a secret and lived like a woman who has to be care-ful."

Shuddering and screeching, about to be born.

"My parents," Catherine whispered.

"What, Catherine?"

"My parents."

"What did she say?" Tom's voice; an irritating buzz, like a horsefly.

A murmur from Randall.

"I thought they died in a car wreck." Tom, clearer now.

"They were murdered," said Catherine.

꧁꧂

"And you think Leona's death ties in with theirs?" Randall asked quietly.

His voice steadied her.

"Oh yes, I think it has to be connected," she said.

Tom looked bewildered, and angry about his bewilderment. They were talking about something he hadn't found out yet.

"Their car was tampered with," she told him. "They were on their way to spend the weekend with me. I was working at a weekly paper in Arkansas, my first job out of college . . . After they crossed the bridge into Arkansas, their car went out of control. Something—" and here Catherine, incurably machine-stupid, shook her head helplessly—"something was loosened with a wrench, deliberately. The Arkansas police investigated the service station they had stopped at there. Sheriff Galton looked here."

"They never caught who did it?" Tom was incredulous.

"No," she said bleakly. "How could they? Anyone could have gotten into our garage, Father didn't lock it. And it must have been done here. Why would a service-station attendant in Arkansas do anything like that? They were nice people . . . I met them."

She closed her eyes and leaned back against the couch.

She heard Tom rise, and knew it was because he was too excited to sit. I've made one person happy today, she thought.

"I'm going to call Galton," he said eagerly. Without another word, he stalked out the back door.

She forgot him as soon as he was gone.

I've been waiting for this, Catherine realized. Somewhere in this little town he's been waiting, too, free and *alive*. Everyone forgot about my parents after a while. But now that he's killed again, he's drawn attention to himself. I've been waiting . . . She knew it now and was amazed she had not known it before. She was frightened to discover that this blood lust existed in quiet Catherine Linton.

But it was anger released. It felt good.

She opened her eyes to meet Randall's. He looked thoughtful.

"Go to bed," he advised gently, and kissed her on the cheek. "I'll come by tomorrow."

She could hear him let himself out as she went obediently to the soft waiting bed. She didn't wonder at his sliding into the position of man to her woman, instead of employer to employee. She accepted the transition without question. As she turned over on her stomach and wrapped her arms around the pillow, she was able to forget her parents, forget Leona Gaites, for the moment before sleep swamped her.

5

CATHERINE SLEPT DREAMLESSLY until morning. She woke slowly; saw early morning light seeping through the curtains, heard birds twittering faintly outside.

She felt weak but at peace, the way an invalid feels after a long and debilitating illness has passed its crisis. She turned on her side to peer out the gap in the curtains, and when she had absorbed what she could see of the morning, her gaze transferred to the curtains themselves.

They were an olive green to match the bedspread. It dawned on Catherine that she didn't like them, had never liked them. In fact, she hated olive green.

She would pick out new curtains, drive to Memphis and debate her choice with a saleswoman at an expensive shop.

I'll buy something light and striped and open-weave. I'll do it this weekend, she resolved. She swung out of bed and went to the louver-doored closet lining one wall of the bedroom. Her supply of clothes, most dating from her college days, barely filled one side of the vast closet.

And I'll buy new clothes, too, she thought. Shoes. She eyed her bedroom slippers with disgust. How could she have kept those for so long?

She went down the dim hall to the kitchen, looking forward to her breakfast. It wasn't until she saw the coffee pot, still dirty from the previous morning, that she remembered.

She sat abruptly on one of the bamboo chairs grouped around the breakfast table. She saw a hand lying in a pool of sunlight. Taking several deep breaths, she focused on the pattern of her robe until the worse had passed. With an immense and grim effort Catherine washed the coffee pot, filled it, and plugged it in. From the pile of library books in the living room, she picked an innocuous biography of an Edwardian lady and sat at the glass-and-bamboo table reading the first paragraphs very carefully until the coffee had perked. After she had poured her first cup, she returned to the book.

She staved off the image of Leona's hand until she had finished three cups of coffee, two pieces of toast, and fifty pages of the lady's opulent childhood.

Then she moved to her favorite chair at the bay window and set herself to think.

If Leona's death was connected with the murder of her parents, what could the connection be? Leona and her mother had never been friends. So Leona and her father, nurse and doctor, must have seen, or found out . . . something to be killed for.

If that was so, if the two had died because they knew the same thing, had seen the same thing (whatever), why the gap in time between the murders? Catherine asked herself. Could Leona have been so difficult to kill that six months had lapsed before the murderer had had another chance?

She shifted restlessly. Hers was not the kind of intelligence that asserted itself in orderly trains of reasoning but the kind that mulled in secret and then presented her, so to speak, with a conclusion.

Instead of undertaking the calm application of logic she had set herself to perform, she found herself dwelling with resentment on the suspicion in

James Galton's face when he told her that the dead woman was Leona Gaites. When Catherine's restlessness goaded her into the bedroom to begin dressing, she was still gnawing at the shock that suspicion had made her feel.

While she was brushing her teeth, Catherine decided she was arrogant.

Why should he *not* suspect her? In all the mystery novels she had read, the finder-of-the-body was suspect.

I never realized how much pride I take in being who I am, she thought. I expect my lineage to speak for me; I think "Scott Linton" means "above reproach." The "Catherine"—that's the important part. That's just me.

She looked in the mirror over the sink and surveyed the toothpaste surrounding her mouth in a white froth.

"Gorgeous," she muttered. "Like a mad dog."

The word *mad* triggered another train of thought. Perhaps Sheriff Galton thought she was seriously crazy? Not just neurotic, but psychotic?

The anger she felt at the possibility was another confirmation, to Catherine's mind, of her own arrogance. She rinsed out her mouth with unnecessary force.

Of course, she brooded, she had reacted drastically

to her parents' deaths. Who wouldn't? Especially when that loss was simultaneously double, untimely, and violent. A period of grief; natural, expected.

But people *had* begun to wonder—she had seen it in their faces, in their careful selection of topics—when the way she lived, holed up in her family home, became permanent. No invitations in, no invitations out. And by the time she realized how she had isolated herself, she had gotten used to it.

I've been working on it, she thought defensively.

The terrible jolts of the day before had shown her how far she had come and how far she had to go.

Like an arrogant fool, I didn't think anyone else would ever hold it to my discredit, she told her reflection silently (she was by now putting on her makeup).

Catherine glared at the mirror and made a horrendous crazy face at herself.

But Randall likes me, she reminded herself.

She picked delicately at the edges of that undeniable fact, half frightened. She mulled over the unexpected feeling that had passed between them.

Then she scolded herself, You're mooning like a fifteen-year-old. And she smoothed her face out and gave the mirror her best, her Number One, smile. It had been a long time since she had used it; it made her cheeks ache.

Instead of donning a long-ago boyfriend's football jersey, which lay at the top of the pile, she rooted deep in a drawer and pulled out something that fit quite a bit better.

The bells of the Baptist church were pealing for the eleven-o'clock service as she put in her earrings.

The church bell chimed in with the doorbell. Catherine opened the front door uncertainly, half doubtful she had heard it.

She had tentatively hoped it would be Randall. It was a dash of cold water in the face to see Sheriff Galton.

⁂

Oh, go away, she told him silently. I had gotten all settled, and here I am mad again.

"I'm sorry to bother you on a Sunday, Catherine, but I've thought of a few more questions I want to ask you."

Galton looked as immovable as a transport truck.

Suddenly Catherine was no longer angry. She felt flat and depressed. She saw in James Galton the grinning man who had swept her to the ceiling in a deliciously frightening game, when he and his wife came to visit Glenn and Rachel Linton.

There was nothing fun about being frightened

now. There was nothing fun about being the sheriff, either. James Galton's face had been sanded down with exhaustion.

"Please come in," she said quietly, standing aside.

He sank down onto the couch with a barely audible sigh of relief. Catherine took the chair Tom had occupied the afternoon before.

For a minute or two they were silent. Galton was lost in some dark alley of thought. Catherine watched him, lit a cigarette, tried to relax. The feeling of being fifteen and in first crush had utterly died away, leaving her hardened, old, and alone. She resolved to behave like a normal, sane, balanced woman—a resolution that immediately made her nervous and fidgety.

"Well, I'll keep this as short as I can," the sheriff began. "I know you probably want to be by yourself"—and Catherine winced as her idea of her image in Lowfield was confirmed— "but you know, Catherine, I don't enjoy this."

She felt remorseful, receptive, and wary, all at once.

"Now, when you were driving to the shack yesterday, did you see anyone you know, anyone at all?"

Catherine reflected obediently.

"No. Well, yes I did," she said, surprised. A blue

pickup had been coming toward Lowfield as she was going to the shack. She remembered a friendly wave through a bug-spattered windshield.

"I saw Martin Barnes," she said without thinking, still amazed that she had forgotten, especially since the sheriff had asked her who rented the land. Was she getting Martin Barnes in trouble? He was a pleasant, not-too-bright man with a married daughter, Sally, who was Catherine's age.

Well, Mr. Barnes is old enough to watch out for himself, Catherine decided with a new tartness.

"What was he driving?" Galton asked.

"His blue pickup. I don't know makes and models. But it was him; he waved at me."

"Where do you reckon you were when you saw him?"

Catherine thought back. Her morning before she had entered the shack was blurry to her now.

"He was fixing to turn onto the highway, just as I was turning off," she said. "You know, there are a couple of houses there. One that Jewel Crenna rents. The other one's empty now."

"The turn-off to the shack," Galton observed mildly.

"Yes," said Catherine and took a deep breath. Despite her every-man-for-himself resolution, she was still dressing things up. She didn't want to point any fingers.

Galton said intuitively, "Catherine, *someone* did this. Maybe someone you know."

"And maybe it was you," whispered the silence that fell after he spoke.

"How long since you saw Leona?" he asked abruptly.

"Tom and Randall asked me that yesterday," she said nervously. "I honestly don't remember."

Do drag in the word "honestly," she congratulated herself savagely. By *all means*.

"If you mean saw her around town," she rattled on, "I guess a couple of weeks ago in the drugstore. If you mean saw her to speak to, it was a few months ago—about three months—when Tom was going to move into the house in back, Father's old office. She called me—" Catherine stopped short.

"She called you?" nudged Galton.

"Yes," Catherine said slowly. "It was really kind of strange. Miss Gaites said she had heard that some-one was moving into the old office, and she knew there were some things in there that Jerry Selforth hadn't wanted to buy. She wanted to know if I needed help moving them."

Catherine remembered smothering her dislike, to

preserve the false face of friendliness she and Leona had always worn when they dealt with each other.

A waste of time, Catherine thought now. And it had been funny-peculiar, her calling like that.

Catherine really had needed help getting those filing cabinets up the collapsible folding stairs that let down from the attic in her father's old office. And she had still been suffering from the "be nice to Leona, she has no family" syndrome. So she had accepted Leona's help with protestations of gratitude.

Though why someone with no family would care to haul heavy things up flimsy stairs, any more than a person with seventy relations, is more than I can figure out, she said to herself.

"What did you talk about that day, Catherine?" asked Galton.

"Well." She hesitated. "The largest things that had to be moved were filing cabinets that Father kept patient files in. Some people still haven't asked for their files, to take over to Jerry's new office. Leona was saying how nice it was that some people were so healthy that they hadn't needed their records for such a long time; that now that the files were going up in the attic, it would be a lot of trouble when someone finally got sick and realized she had to have her records . . . I think I asked Leona if she had applied to be Jerry's nurse; and she said no, she had heard he had a friend who was getting the job, a girl who was going to commute from Memphis. That's all I remember."

The sheriff's only response was a small movement of his huge hand. Catherine wondered if he had been listening. Then she thought clearly, He's trying to decide how to ask me something.

Catherine grew nervous at this hiatus and lit a cigarette. To break the silence, she asked quietly, "How did she die?"

"She died in her house," Galton said heavily. "She was beaten to death. With something rounded and heavy; like a baseball bat.

Catherine went very still and bit the inside of her mouth. Anything she could say would be inadequate.

"Catherine."

Her eyes were blurry with tears of shock. She blinked and Galton came into focus again. She was warned by the sharpness in his face. Something important was coming up.

"Did you sell any of your father's equipment to Leona?"

If she had formed any idea of what Galton's question would be, that was not it.

"What? Why would Leona want anything from the office? I sold almost everything to Jerry."

"What *didn't* you sell to Jerry?"

"Besides those filing cabinets in the attic—"
Catherine made an effort to concentrate, but she was
too confused to remember. "Leona knew. She did all
that, made the list for the lawyer. Father's estate. I
was too upset," Catherine said miserably. She had
always felt some guilt for shoving the task off on
Leona, though Leona had certainly been more quali-
fied to do it. "Maybe there's still the list of stuff for
the lawyer? That you could check against what Jerry
has now?"

Galton didn't comment on her weak suggestion, or
explain why he had asked her, she noticed uneasily;
but the mention of estates had given her something to
chew on.

"Is there anything I ought to do? About Leona's
house? Or about having her buried? She didn't have
any kin, you know." Catherine hated to offer, but knew
she had to. It was the least and last thing she could do
for Leona.

"Her lawyer, John Daniels, will handle all that,
Catherine. She left a will. It's a few years old; and it's
kind of surprising," Galton said smoothly. "She left
everything—house, money—to your father. Now, I
guess, it'll come to you. John Daniels says for you to
call him."

"Shit," said Catherine. "Is that what this is all about?" She was angry now, red hot. "Come on, Sheriff! Leona didn't have doodly-squat. I know Father paid her what he could, but that wasn't all that much; and she hasn't worked since he died."

"As a matter of fact," Galton said calmly, "Leona had quite a bit of money. But she was kind of informal about it. She had little wads stashed all over the house. The only thing she bothered to put in her checking account was her social security check and a little income from a pension plan she belonged to through some nurses' association.

"And," Galton continued, his eyes searching Catherine's face, "someone else besides me knows that. Sometime Friday night, before you found Leona Saturday morning, someone took his time searching Leona's house: either before or after carrying her out to that shack on your place. Your inheritance is a little depreciated. Mattress slashed, chairs ripped open. But the money, and a few other peculiar things, are still there. Strange kind of thief. Didn't kill Leona for her money, but he looked mighty hard for something in her house after he—or she—killed her."

Catherine shook her head. "I don't know; no, I don't *understand* what you mean. If you think"—and her flame of anger flashed through the smoke of bewilderment—"I killed Leona for money, I hate to say this, but you're crazier than I am. I can't believe we're sitting here talking about this. I've known you all my life. My father left me lots of money; my mother left me lots of money; there was insurance besides, and we—I—own the land. In fact, I'm a rich woman. I did not bash Leona on the head so I could come into her bits of money. I did not search her house to make her death mysterious. And if you think I"—and the sweep of her hand down her body pointed out its smallness—"could or would pick up a baseball bat or something, and beat a woman twice my size to death with it, you're just plain damn dumb."

She sank back in her chair feeling clean. Something like a flushed toilet, she told herself bluntly and inelegantly.

Galton was eyeing her with amazement and a reluctant grin.

"I guess you let me have it with both barrels," he said.

Catherine hoped he would add, "Of course I don't think you had anything to do with Leona's murder."

But he didn't.

"Why move the body at all?" she asked out of the blue. It was a point that had been bothering her.

Moving Leona seemed an added risk. There was the chance that someone would see the murderer putting the body in his vehicle. And there was the undeniable conspicuousness of anyone at all being around and about in Lowfield in the late hours of the night. Though Friday night was comparatively busy, that didn't mean much.

"I've been thinking about that," said the sheriff, sounding almost friendly. "And I reckon whoever killed Leona was just trying to delay discovery of her body for as long as possible. She had plenty of neighbors. They would've noticed, after a couple of days of this weather, that something was wrong. But since she kept herself apart, they might not think about not seeing her for quite some time, if the body wasn't there to let them know."

"Maybe someone just couldn't bear to see her lying there after she was dead," Catherine said quietly, her hands running over the carved rosewood of the chair. "And moved her so he wouldn't have to look at her while he searched. It had to be someone strong, didn't it?"

"Yes," Sheriff Galton said, recrossing his legs. He shifted on the soft couch, and sighed. "It was probably a man; maybe a woman, a tall woman, from the angle of the blows."

She had never before been glad she was short.

"Or two people," added the sheriff carefully. He lit a cigarette and leaned forward. "You think to wonder what the killer was searching for, Catherine?"

She shook her head.

"Why, Leona was blackmailing people. She had another career going, but her main line was blackmail. We'll burn what we found so far—after we question the people involved. Just little pieces of nasty evidence she was holding for ransom; none of it criminal material. It's her other career that concerns us even more."

After this revelation, Catherine was literally speechless. She could only wait for Galton to continue. His eyes were resting on her intently, and she felt her hands begin to shake.

"I have one more question to ask you, then I'll leave you to your Sunday," Galton said heavily. "Have you gone to Leona with . . . any kind of *problem*? Since your folks died?"

Catherine felt like a mouse being played with by a big old cat. Her thoughts were slow. She stubbed out her cigarette as she tried to recall, though she was sure she had never taken a problem of any kind to Leona. Her mind wandered. She tried to imagine herself crying on Leona's shoulder over some girlish difficulty, and decided that tears would have just rolled off that starched white shoulder.

When she looked at Galton again, she realized her long pause had cost her something. There was once again a look of sternness in his face.

That's not fair, she thought despairingly.

"I would never take a problem to Leona," she said. Her voice was as weary and watchful as Galton's. Even to her own ears, she sounded unconvincing.

"I thought it would be better if you didn't come down to the station again," Galton murmured. There was a sadness, a regret, in his voice. He too was remembering the days he had swung her up in the air.

Catherine gave up trying. She had done her best, had cleared herself as thoroughly as she could. There was something, or perhaps several things, that Galton wouldn't tell her. He had obviously figured she would be more open in her own home, in a private conversation; he had made a concession to her in that respect. Somehow she had failed to meet his standards.

"I don't know what you want me to tell you. I honestly think"—Do drag in "honestly," Catherine!—"I have told you what little I know. And I think what happened to Leona is directly related to what happened to my parents. I don't blame you for never finding out about them," she added hastily. "I know you were a good friend to my father."

She had touched him on the quick. She wondered if she had meant to.

"I tried," said Galton bitterly. "You're damn right I tried! But I know why Leona Gaites was killed: she was a blackmailer, and something else too. And that doesn't have anything to do with Glenn and Rachel."

He sat silent for a moment, visibly collecting himself. He looked so sad and worn that Catherine was unwillingly moved.

"You need some rest," she said shortly.

"It'll be a while before I get any," he said.

He rose, stretched, ambled to the door.

"Catherine," he said, one hand on the knob, "Why didn't you leave town, honey? What's kept you here?"

"You know, I've asked myself that just recently," she said. "I only found out yesterday. When I was telling Tom Mascalco what happened to Mother and Father. I want the person who did it to be caught. And I want him to be dead. That's why I stayed."

"That Mascalco's a pest," said Galton. "His idea of his job is way too big. About that other, Catherine: it makes me sick to say it—you know how I felt about your folks—but I don't think we'll ever catch who did it. There's nothing for you here. You shouldn't have stayed—if you want unasked-for advice, too late."

The complexity of being sheriff and suspect, family friend and bereaved daughter, tore at them.

"You be careful," he said finally. "I don't know what you've done, or what you know. I've known you to do some things that people thought were crazy. Well, in the Delta we've got a lot of crazies; known for it. Or maybe I should say *eccentrics*. Okay. But I've never known you to be bad or crooked. There's a lot of crookedness, a lot of badness, mixed up in this mess. So watch yourself, Catherine."

He shut the door behind him.

She didn't know whether she'd been threatened or warned.

6

S HE WAS WATCHING the sheriff's car back out
into the street when her telephone rang. Maybe
that's Randall, she thought.

"Catherine?"

"Sally?" Catherine asked uncertainly. She pulled
out one of the bamboo-and-chrome dinette chairs and
sat down heavily.

"Sure is, honey. I'm so sorry for you! You should
have come and spent the night with us! I know you
were scared out of your wits."

How long had it been since she had talked to Sally
Barnes? Sally Barnes Boone, Catherine corrected
herself.

"I'm fine," Catherine said, and made a face into

71

the glass of the table. Once polite lies got into your blood, you never quit telling them, she thought.

"Well, I heard at church," Sally was saying, "and I just couldn't believe it . . . that poor woman! Daddy was so upset, that she was on that land he rents from you! He'd been riding the place that morning, but not close to that field, so he didn't see anything. I just can't imagine who could have done it. Someone from Memphis, I bet. Going through town to the fishing camps at the river."

"I guess so," said Catherine, who didn't think so at all. "How is Bob?" She remembered, almost too late, that Sally had a child. "And the baby?" A little girl, was it?

"Oh, they're fine, just fine. Chrissy's cutting teeth."

"I know she's fretful," Catherine said sympathetically. She had heard somewhere that this was the case with teething babies.

"Oh boy," Sally answered feelingly. "But I want to know about *you*. How are you? What have you been doing? I can't believe I never see you in a town this size!"

Because I have been taking care not to be seen, she thought to herself. I have been waiting.

She could hear a baby's wail in the background, on Sally's end of the line.

"Sally, thanks for calling, I really appreciate it," Catherine said hastily. "But really, I'm not scared. I just happened to find . . ." she trailed off. "But it's not like it was in my *yard* or anything. I'll be fine. Thanks again. I can tell you need to go."

The baby's wails were reaching a crescendo of pique.

"Chrissy, hush!" Sally said faintly. "Bob, pick her up!" Sally's voice grew louder. "Oh, Catherine, I better go, but you come see me real soon. I mean it, now!"

"Sure will. Tell Bob I said hello," and Catherine hung up.

She absently noted that the top of the table was smeared. Her fingernails tapped along the glass as she considered what Sally had said. So Martin Barnes had lied to his daughter. He had said he had been out riding his place. Well, that was possible; every planter rode his acres, looking and assessing. But he had been near the shack where Leona's body was lying. And Catherine had the impression that Mr. Barnes had not been driving from the direction of the shack but had pulled out from one of the houses by the highway. She tried to recall exactly what she had seen. No: she couldn't picture precisely where the truck had been before she passed it.

Catherine shook her head. It was a stupid lie that Martin Barnes was telling. She could see no reason for it; he should have known she would report seeing him. Mr. Barnes was a good planter, but definitely not the smartest of men.

Maybe he was the guilty one. If he was not the guilty man . . . her mouth twisted. This was loathesome. She wanted someone to be proved guilty; fast, so no more suspicion would be attached to her. But she couldn't bear the certain knowledge that the murderer was someone she knew, someone whose face formed a part of her life. She had always known that, but she had never been able to accept it. She couldn't think of anyone in Lowfield she imagined capable of beating a woman to death. Or of loosening an essential part in the car of the town's best-known and most-loved doctor and his wife.

Could it be that Lowfield contained two murderers? That the deaths of her parents and Leona were not related? Sheriff Galton clearly believed the crimes were separate.

A familiar tension, resulting from the suspense of watching and waiting, caused Catherine's muscles to tighten. She simply couldn't picture someone she knew plotting the horrible death Glenn and Rachel Linton had suffered.

Her hand came down flat and hard on the glass.

It left a print, and she retreated into wondering for the hundredth time why her mother had bought a glass-topped table. Catherine had gotten out the glass cleaner and a rag, turning with relief to the mundane little task, when she remembered telling Galton she was a rich woman. She shook her head again.

That was something you just didn't say.

The doorbell rang as Catherine was twisting her neck to look through a shaft of sun, checking to see if she had gotten all the marks off the table.

Does everyone in town want to talk to me? she wondered crossly. For a well-known recluse, I'm having lots of company these days.

Molly Perkins, the coroner's wife, was standing with a casserole dish clutched in her hands when Catherine opened the door. Catherine had automatically looked up, and she had to adjust her sights down to meet Miss Molly's washed-blue eyes.

Miss Molly began instantly. "I am *so* sorry you had such a *horrible* experience. I know you're upset. I won't stay but a minute, I just wanted to run this over to you. I knew you wouldn't feel like cooking."

Food, the southern offering on the altar of crisis. Catherine was bemused by its presentation now.

Finding a corpse must be close enough to death in the family to qualify.

"Thanks," she said faintly. "Please come in."

"Well, like I say, I won't stay but a minute. I know you must be busy with company coming by and all."

The plump little woman was trotting through the living room back to the kitchen.

"Company?" Catherine asked the air behind her.

But Mrs. Perkins apparently didn't hear her.

Molly Perkins's whole body tilted forward when she walked, giving her the effect of charging eagerly forward at life. Her enormous bosom made her appear in danger of falling flat on her face at any moment, which had added a pleasant suspense to her company when Catherine was younger.

Placing the casserole on the kitchen counter, Mrs. Perkins earnestly continued, "I do hope you like gumbo. All these years up here, and I still cook Cajun. I always fix too much for Carl and myself. I just got used to cooking a lot while Josh was growing up. Can't change my habits now he's married and gone, I guess."

"Thank you," Catherine said again, determined to get a word in somewhere. "And how is Josh?"

"We got a phone call from him and his wife Friday," said Miss Molly happily. "They're expecting.

Carl is so excited. About that, and Josh is doing well in L.A."

"I know Mr. Perkins is proud of him," Catherine murmured. Her conversation with Perkins at the tenant shack was the only one she could remember that didn't feature Josh: his job, his wife (beautiful and of good family), and his brilliant prospects.

"I do wish they were settled here," Mrs. Perkins said wistfully. "That's why we built that big house. Not many young people do stay in Lowfield, seems like."

Catherine slid the gumbo dish back against the wall. She couldn't think of anything to say. As she remembered Josh, who was a few years older, the last thing he'd do would be to settle down quietly in Lowfield.

"I thought I saw a police car here this morning. I hope you haven't had any trouble?" asked Molly Perkins with a forced air of casualness.

So that was the "company"; that was the purpose of this visit. The food, Catherine thought quickly, was an excuse to unearth interesting facts to relate at the beauty parlor.

"No," said Catherine calmly. "No trouble."

Against the stone wall of Catherine's face, the little woman was visibly stymied.

"I guess Jimmy Galton has been mighty busy," she said nervously.

"I imagine," said Catherine.

The ensuing silence lasted a moment too long to be comfortable. Damned if I'll break it, Catherine thought.

"Well, I've got to be getting back; I hope you enjoy that gumbo."

And Mrs. Perkins trotted top-heavily to the front door, with Catherine again trailing behind.

"I got a post card from the Drummonds," Mrs. Perkins said abruptly.

"Oh?"

"They're in Florence, Italy. They'll be back in another week," Mrs. Perkins offered. "They're having a wonderful time, they say."

Catherine nodded.

"Well, I hope you enjoy the gumbo," Mrs. Perkins repeated desperately.

"I'm sure I will." She noticed that Molly Perkins did not offer the quick hug and kiss that was customary on food-bringing visits.

"Can't let all your air conditioning run out the door!" Mrs. Perkins concluded with artificial gaiety.

And off she trotted with an anxious backward glance at Catherine, who remained in the doorway with her arms folded across her chest until the woman had gotten down the walkway and turned right to cross the street to her own house.

When Miss Molly had entered the mansion's front door, Catherine slammed her own violently. "Talk talk talk," she muttered. Miss Molly had come to spy and pry, to report on Catherine's mental state and demeanor. And yet Catherine knew the pigeon-breasted little lady had also been genuinely worried about her well-being.

The phone rang as Catherine stood in the middle of the living room brooding over this duality in small-town life. She was bitterly sure the caller was not Randall: How could it be? That was who she wanted to talk to. She decided it was another sympathy call from some high school classmate she hadn't seen in years.

The irritating sound served to trigger the anger Galton and Molly Perkins had generated. Catherine said something that undoubtedly shocked the very curtains in her mother's living room. She had never in her life been able to take a telephone off the hook. The alternative was to leave the telephone. Catherine marched out her back door and across the lawn to Tom's house.

She pounded, rather than knocked, on the back door.

She was holding her heavy hair up off her neck, to take advantage of a slight breeze—maybe it would cool her down—when Tom answered. He was almost as surprised to receive a visit from Catherine as she was to be making one.

She had not entered the old office since Tom had moved in.

"Well, the landlady comes to call," he said easily, opening the screen door for her to enter. "Just come this way through the foyer, and don't scuff the marble."

Catherine looked around as she went through the hall. Dr. Linton's office had been a house before he bought it; now it was a house again. Her father had used the rooms at the back of the old house for examinations and storage. They were now Tom's kitchen and bedrooms. The living room had been Dr. Linton's waiting room; now it had cycled back. Catherine took stock of the reversion.

"You recognize, of course, my furniture period— Modern American Battered."

Tom's description was accurate. His couch and chairs were covered with mismatched throws, to hide the worst holes from sight—but not from sensation, as Catherine found when she sat down.

But the place was neater than she had expected. The couch, where Tom obviously had been lying, had a sad old trunk exactly centered before it to serve as a coffee table. On the trunk was a neat pile of magazines, a telephone aligned with the pile, and what Catherine supposed was a cigarette box beside a large cheap ashtray.

"You keep it nice," Catherine offered.

"Oh, Mother Mascalco brought her boy up right," Tom said with a grin. She noticed that Tom wasn't sloppy in dress even on the weekend. He was wearing a sports shirt obviously straight from the laundry; and, amazingly, his jeans had creases. "The bed, I have to admit, is not made. You wouldn't be interested in seeing the bedroom?"

Catherine shook her head with a smile. "We wouldn't suit," she said. "Besides, what happened to your fiancée in Memphis? I thought one reason you took the job here was because you could drive up to see her on weekends."

"She dumped me," Tom said, with an attempt at lightness. "Haven't you noticed that I've been lurking around here the past two weekends?"

Well, yes, she had noticed, kind of. But she had vaguely assumed he had fetched the girl from Memphis for some weekend housekeeping. Tom's visits to her house had been during the past two weeks, now that she came to think of it.

"Stuck here for nothing," Catherine said, making a tactful effort to match Tom's light tone. "Well, this job will look good on your résumé."

"Yeah," he said morosely. "Want something to drink? Beer, orange juice? I have some milk, too," he added apologetically, "but I think it's past its prime. Or dope?" He opened the cigarette box, and Catherine saw that it held at least fifteen rolled joints.

"Yes to the beer," she said.

"Turning into an alcoholic," Tom said with a mocking shake of the head, as he unfolded his lanky frame from the low couch and went into the kitchen.

"You better watch out with this stuff," Catherine called after him, putting the lid back on the cigarette box. She wandered around the room, then followed him to the kitchen. It too was neat, without being exactly clean. "This little house sits in the county, you know," she said "and you'd have Galton to contend with rather than the town police."

"You can't be serious," he said incredulously. "Why isn't the road in front of this house the city limit? There's only cotton fields on the other side of it! I feel like a planter every time I go out the front door!"

"I don't know," Catherine said. She was looking around the kitchen, which her father had used for the shelving of medicines and supplies of plastic gloves and tongue depressors. The little stool Leona had used to get supplies from the top shelf was still sitting by the door. "The line runs right through my backyard."

Tom shook his head darkly at this piece of town planning, and Catherine wandered back out into the living room. The office—the house, she corrected herself—was as familiar to her as her own home, and it felt strange being a guest in it.

She sat down in the caved-in chair and leaned forward to see what magazines Tom bought. A photography glossy, *Playboy, Time.* The phone placed so neatly by the stack was a princess type. On the smooth back of the receiver Tom had pasted a list of phone numbers. It was not an extensive list. Tom was not integrated into the town's life yet, since he had been gone on weekends for the past months. Catherine noted that her own number topped the list. He really *doesn't* know any girls, she thought wryly.

But Tom was attractive in a long dark way, and Leila, the *Gazette* secretary-receptionist, had been giving him the eye ever since he started work. With the fiancée out of the picture, maybe Tom would wake up to Leila's adoring brown eyes.

"How did your dad stand having his office and

house so close?" he asked as he handed Catherine her can of beer.

"The house I live in now was my grandparents'," she explained. "When my dad finished medical school and moved back in with them, they were already getting old. They had him late, and he was an only child. So he wanted to be close to them in case of an emergency, and my mother didn't mind living with them. This house was up for sale. So it was convenient to him." She sighed. "Things were different then. People would come at night—" and Catherine stopped dead.

She rose abruptly and walked straight to the door leading to the hall. She examined the door frame.

"Termites?" Tom asked silkily.

"Smartass," Catherine said with irritation. "No, look at this."

He joined her.

"It's a buzzer, like a doorbell, and it rings in the master bedroom in my house. Dad had it put in so that if emergencies came at night, people could come into this waiting room and buzz him. I told you things were different then. He left the front door unlocked, only locked this door opening into the hall. I had completely forgotten about it."

"My God, you mean I could ring for you?" Tom leered theatrically.

"Yes, but you'd better not!"

"It still works?"

"I guess so," said Catherine, dismayed. "Now don't go playing jokes on me, you hear?"

For a moment Tom looked as mischievous as an eight-year-old with a frog in his pocket. Then his thin lips settled into an unusual line of sobriety.

"No, I promise, Catherine," he said. "You've had enough shocks."

"Thank you," Catherine said with feeling. She sat back down.

Tom lit a joint. "Sure you don't want some? Make you feel better," he advised her.

She shook her head. "Did you buy that here?" she asked curiously.

"Yes," he answered, after he expelled the smoke he had been holding deep in his lungs. "The other night. My first Lowfield dope run."

"Not from Leona, surely?" Catherine asked impulsively.

"Christ, no!" Tom stared at her. "What the hell made you think that?"

But Catherine didn't want to tell him that the sheriff had hinted that Leona had had something from her father's office—presumably medical equipment. She felt foolish for even thinking of Leona as a marijuana processor. Did you need medical things to prepare it to smoke? She could see Tom worrying over her rash question like a dog with an especially meaty bone.

"Come on, honey, you know something," Tom coaxed.

He's sure not short on charm when he wants something, Catherine told herself. Tom had a convincing way of fixing his heavily lashed brown eyes on a potential source of information with melting effect; but Catherine had seen the trick too many times to be swayed.

"Save that for Leila," she said callously.

"Leila?" Tom asked. "What is this about Leila?"

His vanity, so badly bruised by his fiancée, was fully aroused. Catherine could tell she wasn't going to get out of answering his question.

"Oh, she likes you," she said reluctantly, regretting she had introduced the subject. "I can't believe you haven't noticed it." But he hadn't, that was plain. He stroked his villainous mustache in a pleased way.

"She's a pretty girl," he said thoughtfully.

"And just out of high school, and never been out of Lowfield," Catherine said warningly. Now shut up, she told herself. You've already made one mistake.

She didn't want to compound it by being fosterer and confidant to a relationship she thought would surely end in trouble. Tom was vain and immature; and Leila was too far gone on him before any relationship had even begun, and so very young.

Who am I, God? Catherine asked herself harshly. Quit predicting. You're not exactly the world's authority on men and women. How many dates have *you* had lately?

"Didn't you go out on Friday?" she asked Tom, changing the subject so she could stop feeling guilty. "Have a date?"

"No," he said sharply.

"I wasn't spying," she said indignantly. "I heard your car, and you know how hard it is to mistake any other car for yours." (A defensive jab; Tom's Volkswagen was notably noisy.) "I noticed it because I was trying to go to sleep."

Tom relaxed in a cloud of pungent smoke. "Sure you won't have some of this?"

"No," she said impatiently.

"It's pretty good stuff for homegrown," he said. "No, I didn't have a date. I went out to buy this. It's not easy to set up when you don't know anybody. Took me forever."

"Did you see—anything?" Leona had been killed Friday night, the doctors said.

"What do you mean?"

"I don't know, Tom. Anything?"

"You know what Lowfield is like on Friday night. I saw the high school kids riding around and around over the same streets. I saw the blacks who live out in the country coming into town to drink. I barely saw Cracker Thompson" (who was something in the position of the village idiot) "riding around on his bicycle without any reflectors, wearing dark clothes. If that's what you mean by 'anything.' I presume," said Tom, drawing out the words lovingly, "you mean, did I see Leona Gaites dragged out of her house screaming, by a huge man with a two-by-four."

Catherine shuddered. Though Sheriff Galton had told her that Leona was beaten to death, the reminder conjured up the same horrible pictures: Leona's outstretched hand; the flies.

Tom observed her shudder with bright eyes. "Jerry told me that something heavy and wooden was probably the weapon, a baseball bat or something like that—the traditional blunt instrument. Anyway"—and Tom hunted around for his point—"no, I didn't see 'anything.' "

Foolish, Catherine said to herself. I was foolish to ask. That must be good dope. Maybe I should have taken it. I could have had hours of entertainment just sitting and laughing to myself.

"But I might have," Tom said suddenly. "Maybe I can use that."

"What do you mean?"

But Tom waved a hand extravagantly and laughed. Catherine eyed him as he slid lower in his seat. His spider legs were sprawled out in front of him. If he relaxes any more he'll pour off that couch, she thought.

"Tom," she said uneasily.

"My lady speaks?"

"Don't . . ." she hesitated. She was not exactly sure of how to put it. "Don't let anyone think you know more than you do."

"Little Catherine!" He grinned at her impishly.

"I'm not kidding, Tom. Look at what happened to my parents. Look what happened to Leona . . . though the sheriff doesn't seem to think it's related." She frowned, still not satisfied that the sheriff was right; though from his mysterious hints she knew there was something about Leona's activities that Galton felt had led directly to her death.

"I know more than James Galton, that's for sure," Tom said, with a whisker-licking effect. "Guess who's selling dope in Lowfield?"

Catherine raised her eyebrows interrogatively.

"Jimmy Galton, Junior!" Tom laughed.

"Oh no," Catherine murmured in real distress. If Tom knew that, who else did? All the kids in Lowfield, of course. Poor Sheriff Galton. Did he know? In his job, how could he avoid knowing? She wondered if Leona had known James Junior's occupation, too. And whether the wads of cash found in Leona's house were hush money paid by one of the Galtons to ensure she kept quiet. Money that was now coming to her, Catherine remembered, sickened.

"I wish you hadn't told me that, Tom," she said bitterly.

"I'll comfort you, little Catherine."

"The hell you will. I'm going home."

"Oh, stay and have another beer." And he gave her his charming grin. "We can pool our resources." His eyebrows waggled suggestively.

"Yeah, sure," she said, laughing in spite of herself. "Right now I don't feel like I have any resources to pool. Thanks for the beer."

Tom made a gentlemanly attempt to rise.

"No, don't get up, you look like you'll fall down if you do. I know where the door is. See you tomorrow."

"Yes," Tom said cheerfully. "I've got to write Leona's obit."

On that happy note, Catherine shut the screen door behind her.

She had to lengthen her stride to hit the stepping-
stones that linked their back doors. The hedges between the houses joined the hedges running down the
sides of the yard, making an H of greenery. Her parents had planted it for privacy from the street on one
side and from neighbors on the other; and to separate
the office and home backyards. It had gotten out of
hand, and Catherine reminded herself, as she went
through the gap planned for her father's passage, that
she needed to take care of it.

I ought to do it myself, she thought. Then she looked
down at her arms, too pink and tender from exposure
to the sun the day before, and decided to hire someone.

What are these bushes, anyway? she wondered. She
rubbed some leaves between her fingers, which of
course told her nothing. She was trying to avoid thinking about the Galtons, Senior and Junior. Catherine
stared at the growth blankly. I hate this damn hedge,
she thought. I'll cut the whole thing down. Both yards
are open anyway, and what do I do in the backyard that
anyone shouldn't see?

The hedge was added to her mental list of things
to change, which already numbered curtains, bedspread, clothes, and shoes.

It made her feel a little better, planning for the fu-
ture.

When all this is over, she thought vaguely.

As she entered her back door, she heard the front doorbell ringing. No rest for the wicked, she told herself grumpily. What'll I get this time? An interrogation? A chicken casserole?

In this disagreeable frame of mind, she swung open the front door. Finally, her caller was Randall.

7

"WANT TO GO out to the levee with me?"

"Okay," Catherine said smoothly, dancing a little jig inside. "Come in while I straighten myself up."

She had only seen him in the conservative suits he wore at the *Gazette*. He was wearing khakis and a T-shirt. He looked incredibly muscular for a newspaper editor. He looked wonderful.

I am smitten, Catherine said silently as she gave her hair a hasty brushing in the bedroom. How long has it been since I was smitten?

She remembered as she touched up her makeup.

She had overheard the young man through her dorm window. He had been talking to a fraternity brother after he had deposited Catherine at the door.

"How was your date with Sphinx?" the fraternity brother had asked idly.

"Like dating Snow White. You never know if she's going to say anything, or if she does, what it's going to be; and you feel like she might have the Seven Dwarves in her pocket."

He had never asked her out again; and Catherine had been too unnerved and hurt to accept a date for a long time after that.

But I'm not scared now, she realized as she dashed into the bathroom (wouldn't do to have to go at the levee).

She wondered, as she flushed the toilet, if Randall was so tempting because she had been so lonely for so long; because Leona's solitary life and death had forced her to wonder if she would be alone forever.

"I don't care," she said out loud, zipping up her blue jeans.

She decided, peering in the mirror again, that she looked positively animated. The sun yesterday had taken care of her need for color. "Though I wish," she muttered, "it had skipped my nose in the process."

What the hell, she thought, stuffing her keys in one pocket and her cigarette case in the other. What the hell.

✦

She had not been prepared to be so relaxed with him. She had heard talk of Randall all her life: her mother had been fond of his mother, though Angel Gerrard was considerably older. The two women, sitting companionably in the kitchen over coffee, had discussed their children; and Catherine, in and out, had heard (without caring a great deal, since he was so much older) of Randall's progress through college, graduate school, and employment with a congressman who was a Gerrard family friend.

Since Catherine had gotten a job at the *Gazette,* Randall had scarcely become more real. His presence had seemed so familiar, in a shadowy way, that she had never looked squarely at him. And during her first weeks of work, Catherine had been functioning automatically, in a state of shock. When her feeling had slowly returned, tingling as if her whole body had been asleep, she had come to know her coworkers bit by bit, but Randall had remained on the outer fringes. He was in and out of the office, selling advertising space, hiring delivery men, supervising the unloading of the enormous rolls of paper for the press: always busy. He was alert to the contents of his paper, writing stories himself when Tom and Catherine had too much on their hands. And always passing through.

He must be as used to hearing my name as I am to hearing his, Catherine thought, as they drove out of town in easy silence. This third-hand familiarity eliminated the need to exchange information immediately, as men and women usually did. Catherine became almost drowsy with comfort.

They were coming to the levee. The graveled road, which had been aiming through the seemingly endless level terrain of the fields, mounted to the levee in a sharp swoop.

She leaned forward a little, reliving the excitement she had felt at this abrupt climb when she was little and riding with her grandfather in his pickup. It had been as thrilling as a roller coaster.

Randall looked over at her and smiled.

A last lurch and they were on top of the levee. The graveled road on the top was barely wide enough for two vehicles to pass. On the river side, the green grass slope was scattered with cattle. It ran down to the trees that marked the edge of the marshy land bordering the river, though in places the slope rose again to modest bluffs that overlooked the water.

Some roads led down to fishing camps. Randall bypassed them, to Catherine's relief. The fishing camps were tawdry and depressing, with their ramshackle weekend cabins and litter of beer bottles.

"Where are we going, Randall?" she asked shyly.

"To the party bluff."

She nodded. That was the right place to go today.

"I haven't been out there since I was in high school," she said. "I hear they've put garbage cans out there, picnic tables. And some gravel to park on."

"Yes," he said. "When I was in high school, someone got stuck out there every spring. We would all be drunk as lords, scrambling around in the mud, trying to find wood to put under the tires. Our parents' cars, of course. Having to drive back into town in someone else's car, trying to get Danny at the Shell station to take his tow truck out there without phoning our folks."

"Pooling your money to pay him," Catherine murmured, nodding.

"Right," Randall laughed, his memories chiming with hers.

They took the turnoff to the bluff. The road plunged down at what seemed an impossible angle. Catherine had a moment to think "roller coaster," and they charged down.

And down. The road, which disintegrated into a graveled track, began winding narrowly through choking undergrowth. The track had been built up to avoid flooding, but after any considerable rain, parts of it were under water. Since the weather had been so dry for so long, they didn't have to worry about that today. Catherine could see the roots of the trees sticking up like bare bones. Branches brushed the car. The road was roofed with interlocking greenery. Inside the car it was cool and dim.

Randall drove very slowly. The gravel had petered out, leaving only dirt, heaved and holed by the rain and then baked hard. The car rocked and shimmied.

After some twists, they began to climb again. The trees thinned, the driving was easier.

Catherine saw the shimmer of the sun on the water.

The bluff had been cleared of trees, leaving a large open area. There was a graveled turnaround, which Randall circled so that the car pointed back down the track. A couple of oil drums had been cleaned and placed in the clearing to hold garbage, and they showed evidence of heavy use.

"Much better," Catherine said approvingly.

She and Randall didn't speak again until they had settled on the edge of the bluff. Below them the bank fell away gently down to the lapping water. The bank was concrete, old and broken in places, allowing the relentless Mississippi weeds to push their heads through the cracks. There was river litter, not human litter, scattered on the concrete—bits of wood and weed.

Catherine sighed. The bank of Arkansas was clear but tiny across the river.

She was content.

This was not like being with any other man. She couldn't explain to herself how someone so distant and so taken for granted could have switched positions so easily and naturally. She didn't want to explain, or worry, or wonder; or try to picture how he saw her. She was, for once, quite unselfconscious.

The swift and treacherous current swept a large branch downriver toward New Orleans. They watched it pass. The river spawned big sweeping thoughts that were best shared silently.

"Maybe a barge will go by," Catherine said, after a time.

When she had been in her teens, a group of them would stand on the bluff and shout to the bargemen, their voices carrying across the river. The bargemen would sometimes sound the deep barge horn in reply.

"It's better at night," Randall observed after a peaceful interval.

She remembered. The lights, shining over the dark water until the barge was out of sight around the bend in the river.

"We'll stay until one comes," he said.

He inched back on his rear until he was behind Catherine, his legs on either side of her. His thick fingers began to work gently in her hair, separating strands, combing them through. Catherine was catlike in her pleasure, her eyes half closed, delight running down her spine.

"It's like a bowl, the rim of a bowl," she murmured. His fingers brushed her scalp and she shivered. "No beginning, no end. The river goes on and on. And kids come out to watch it in the night."

"And barges come down with lights on."

"The cotton grows," she said, "and they harvest it and plant more."

"And there are the same roles to be taken in the town," he said. "Different people assume them. But they all get taken and worked, over and over—mayor, town drunk, planter. Newspaper editor."

"Dogs get hit by cars," she said, her voice sharpening, losing its drowsy dreamy pitch.

"And there are other dogs," Randall said quietly. His hands rested in her hair, still, waiting.

"Other dogs," she agreed after a moment, and his hands began moving.

She had almost lost their moment when she once again saw a large dun-colored dog lying by the side of a dusty road. But the continuity of the river, mirroring the continuity of their town, washed away that picture in its current.

They moved into the shade when Catherine's skin began to prickle. Randall lay under a dilapidated picnic table, reckless of ants and other interested insects. Catherine lay on her stomach on top of the table, peering down at him. She was not afraid of ants, not today, but she wanted to see his face.

"What did you do in Washington?" she asked lazily.

"I gave out the senator's press releases. I told people things. I leaked information on request." He laughed.

"Did you want to come back?"

"Not at first. I had forgotten how it was. I was proud I was a citizen of the bigger world."

"And later?"

"Well," he said more slowly, "I didn't resent the family-legacy thing after a while. Once I got back into living in Lowfield, it all seemed right and natural."

"Do you miss Washington, and being in the center of things? A citizen of the bigger world?"

He thought. Catherine watched the ripple of his muscles as he put his arms behind his head.

"When I've been in Lowfield for a while," he answered slowly, "it seems like the center of things."

"Can you see without your glasses?" Catherine asked solemnly.

"No," said Randall and smiled. He took them off and blinked at her blindly. "Do you get tired of writing up weddings?"

"They're all the same: only the names have been changed," she said. "I like it mostly. It needs to be done, and it keeps me busy. It makes people happy . . . Did you want to hire me?"

"I knew you could do it," Randall said. "I just wondered why you wanted to. Then I talked to my mother, who still has half-interest in the paper. She was absolutely sure that you were exactly what the *Gazette* needed. I think she had designs on you."

Catherine raised her eyebrows.

"She was tired of my catting off to Memphis bars."

"Oh." Catherine blinked.

"Time coasted by, and I was busy and you were quiet and did your work and went home."

Catherine said, "Um."

"And gradually, as I began to remember the reason I thought she wanted you at the paper, I began to look at you."

"I didn't realize."

"I know, and I was mad as hell. I said, 'Randall, you're twelve years older than this girl, and you prance by her desk a dozen times a day, and she doesn't look up. When you talk to her, she just nods and goes back to work.'" He opened his eyes to cock a look at Catherine. She kept her face still. "'And she looks at you blankly,'" he said.

Catherine laughed.

"I practically doubled my running time in the evening and added five pounds to my weights."

She reached down to touch his shoulder appreciatively.

"And I was scared to ask you out, because you were an employee, and how would you feel you could refuse? I didn't know how you'd react."

"You came when I was in trouble," she said. "I see you now."

"This isn't how things usually go," he said.

"I know."

<hr />

They saw their barge.

It swept around the bend in the river, majestic in the night. Its lights shone across the water.

Randall shouted, and the answering sound of the horn drifted, melancholy and beautiful, over the dark moving river.

※

"I have gumbo," Catherine said, on their way back into town.

"It was contributed by Mrs. Perkins; she's from Louisiana, and I'm sure she's an excellent gumbo cook."

"Is that an offer?"

"Yes," she said, shy again since they had left the levee.

"I'm hungry."

The gumbo was excellent.

※

"Shall I stay?" he asked.

The weight of the next day descended prematurely. They would become employer and employee again. Then she couldn't stand herself for letting the thought cross her mind.

She was tempted to say yes, to get all the good out

of this day she could, fearing it might not last, might never happen again. She had not trusted tomorrow for a long time.

She gambled.

"No, let's wait," she said.

8

AFTER THE SHOCK, fear, and joy of the weekend, Monday began badly. Catherine wanted to
wear something she had never worn to the office before, in Randall's honor. But her closet held only the
unexciting shirtwaists she had worn as a freshman
in college, when girls still wore dresses to class. She
had worn them all scores of times.

If Randall and I go out this weekend, I'll have to
go to Memphis one evening this week and buy something to wear, she thought cautiously. I'm damned if
I'll wear one of these.

She pulled on her least-faded dress, in a snit of
anger at herself.

"Morning," she said curtly to Leila Masham as she

entered the *Gazette*'s front door, which faced onto the town square. Her temper was not improved by the sight of long-legged Leila in a brand-new summer dress that bared Leila's golden shoulders. The girl flagged her down with an urgent wave, so Catherine had to stop instead of marching through the reporters' room.

Catherine expected inquiries about the weekend's big incident, but single-minded Leila whispered theatrically, "Tom came in early this morning!" The girl's brown eyes were open wide at this unprecedented beginning to a Monday.

"He didn't have to drive down from Memphis," Catherine whispered back, reminded of Leila's infatuation in time to stop herself from saying, "So what?"

"Was *she* down *here*?"

"She" must be Tom's fiancée.

Leila would have to find out sooner or later.

"They broke up," Catherine said expressionlessly.

She had given Leila the keys to heaven.

"Ooh," Leila said, as if she had been hit on the back.

Catherine shook her head as she crossed the reporters' room to her desk. Tom was hard at work already, typing furiously, taking swift sideways glances at the notes by his typewriter. He acknowledged her with a look and a nod that said he didn't want to be interrupted, and hunched back over the keys. His long thin fingers flew.

"Such activity on a Monday," Catherine muttered, whipping the plastic cover from her own typewriter. Then she realized that Tom was writing what would be the lead story, about Leona's murder. She paused with her hands in her lap, the cover clutched half-folded between her fingers.

I have a lot to do, and this can't get in the way, she told herself sternly. She stuffed the cover into its accustomed drawer with a resolute air, and pulled out a sheaf of papers from her Pending basket. As she flipped through them, she kept an ear cocked for Randall's voice.

Gradually, as she became caught up in her work, she forgot to listen. When that dawned on her, she thought, All to the good.

She was studying the layout of her society page—which she briefly sketched out as it filled up—when she realized with a jolt that Randall was standing at the other side of the desk.

I'm as bad as Leila, she thought ruefully.

"Movie in Memphis Friday night?" he asked.

She nodded.

"Won't you smile, Sphinx?"

She smiled.

As he walked through Leila's room into his office, she typed cheerfully, "The mother of the bride wore beige silk . . ."

⚒

Catherine polished off two weddings with dispatch. She was glad she didn't have to actually attend the ceremonies. She usually dropped by the bride's house and extended her regrets, leaving a form to fill out that made writing the stories practically automatic.

Bridesmaids' names and places of residence, descriptions of everyone's dress, and details of the decorations at the short Southern reception. Groom's employment, bride's employment (this last recently instituted). Honeymoon itinerary.

Summer and Christmas were the wedding seasons. May was parties for graduates. Obituaries and children's birthday parties, anniversary celebrations and dinner parties, trips and out-of-town guests filled up the rest of the year. All of these appeared on Catherine's society page except the obituaries, which were scattered through the paper as fillers. Catherine wrote those as well—unless the death was unusual in some way, in which case Tom picked it up.

Leila buzzed Catherine's extension more often than any other. At the little paper, Monday and Tuesday were the busiest days, the two days before the paper came out, when people realized they had to contact her before the weekly noon deadlines. The *Gazette* was printed on Wednesday morning, distributed Wednesday afternoon.

This Monday was no exception. Catherine worked steadily through the morning, taking notes from callers and typing them up as soon as possible.

By eleven, her desk was an impossible clutter. It was time to review what she had done and what she had left to do. Four weddings. One for this Wednesday's paper, three for the next issue. She carefully dated them. She had taken two more weddings back to the typesetter the previous Friday. She checked: yes, the accompanying pictures were attached to her new copy.

She put the copy in a basket and sorted through the other sheets of flimsy yellow paper. A little social note about the Drummonds' progress in Europe: that should please the old couple when they returned and read the back issues. A bridal shower. A baby shower. And two children's birthday parties. Catherine wrinkled her nose in distaste.

The last society editor had started this practice, and

it was a sure-fire paper seller, but Catherine had always felt it horribly cutesy to write up infants' birthday parties. The stories were invariably accompanied by amateurish pictures taken by doting grandparents: pictures featuring babies sitting more or less upright in highchairs, often with party hats fixed tipsily to their heads. Catherine had long wanted to discontinue this feature, but in view of the papers it sold (every child having multiple relations who were sure to want a copy or two), she had never discussed it with Randall. The *Gazette* needed all the revenue it could get.

The Gerrard family was well enough off, but only because a wise forebear had made it legally impossible to put family money into the paper. Several generations of Gerrards had gotten ulcers achieving solvency for the *Gazette*.

One of the birthday stories for the upcoming issue was complete, with story written and picture attached. The other was written, but there was no picture. Catherine remembered as she read the first line of copy that this was Sally Barnes Boone's baby's party. It had been held at grandfather Martin Barnes's house; and Catherine recalled that Mrs. Barnes had assured her that she would bring the picture in before Monday noon.

Catherine glanced at the clock. Damn, she should

call. But she felt awkward about phoning the Barnes home. They might resent her telling the sheriff about Martin's proximity to Leona's dumped body. Barnes's wife Melba had a reputation for being unpredictable.

I guess she's one of those well-known Delta eccentrics that Sheriff Galton was so proud of, Catherine thought sourly. I'll wait until tomorrow, she equivocated. Maybe someone'll show up with the damn picture.

She hadn't had time to pay attention to what Tom was doing. Now she saw him through the picture window that made the reporters' room a sunny fishbowl. He was striding toward the courthouse, which sat in the center of the square, his camera in hand.

That meant he had already turned in his Leona Gaites story to Jewel Crenna, the typesetter. Catherine wanted to read it, and she had to take her copy back to Production anyway. She gathered up a sheaf of yellow paper and went through the swinging door to the big production room.

It was not exactly silence that met her as the backroom staff observed her entrance, but there was a definite, abrupt halt of activity. Catherine stopped right inside the door, surprised.

They want to ask me all about it, she realized after

a second. No people on earth were as curious as people working in any capacity for a newspaper, she had found after she had started work at the *Gazette*.

Now Catherine straightened her shoulders, set her lips, and refused to meet the glances that sought to stop her.

Garry, the foreman, and Sarah, the senior paste-up girl, wouldn't have the face to accost her directly, Catherine figured rapidly, but she dreaded encountering Salton Sims, the pressman. He would ask anyone *anything* he wanted to know.

Catherine nipped quickly into the typesetter's cubicle. Jewel Crenna was hard at work and notoriously temperamental on Mondays and Tuesdays, so Catherine leaned against the wall behind her without speaking, and scanned Jewel's In basket. It was full to the brim with additions to ads, and last-minute amendments to stories Jewel had set the previous week. Catherine added her own sheaf to the pile and began searching the hook that held processed galleys of type. Jewel would have set Tom's story as soon as it came in, so the staff could read it.

Jewel glanced up once to identify the intruder in her bailiwick, and then her eyes swiveled back to the typed page held by a clamp in front of her, her fingers moving surely and with a speed that Catherine envied.

Jewel was a tall woman with suspiciously black hair and clear olive skin. She was a handsome woman with strong features and a tart tongue that knew no hesitation, a tongue that was widely supposed to be the cause of her two divorces.

Catherine had always had a sneaking admiration for Jewel, well mixed with a healthy fear. Jewel was an uninhibited shouter when she was irritated, and shouting people had always cowed Catherine completely.

Catherine skimmed through the justified type, getting the gist of Tom's well-written account. She raised her eyebrows when she found herself quoted. She hadn't said anything like what Tom had blithely invented. He must have felt free to take liberties since he was quoting a fellow reporter.

Oh well, she shrugged. The quotes were undoubtedly better copy than anything she had actually said; and they were truthful in content, if not in source.

She was so absorbed in reading that it was a while before she realized that Jewel's fingers had stopped moving—an incredible event on a Monday. Catherine looked up to find Jewel facing her, broad hands fixed on her knees.

"I hope I haven't bothered you," Catherine said instantly. She didn't want Jewel to let loose with one of the pithy phrases she used to blast disturbers of her peace. Jewel was aware that she was indeed a gem to Randall and the *Gazette*.

The whine of the press, stopping and starting as Salton Sims overhauled it, made Jewel's cubicle a little corner of isolation.

"I hear you told the police you saw Martin close to where they found that Gaites woman," Jewel said abruptly.

"Yes," Catherine admitted cautiously, wondering at Jewel's interest.

"Now Melba Barnes has got it in her head Martin was out at that shack meeting Leona Gaites for some fun, and found her dead," Jewel said contemptuously. "As if Martin would have anything to do with a plucked chicken like Leona Gaites! That Melba hasn't got the brains God gave a goat." Jewel paused invitingly, but Catherine prudently kept her mouth shut. The light was dawning about Martin Barnes's presence on that road Saturday morning. He hadn't been riding his place at all: he had been at Jewel Crenna's house by the highway.

"Martin's a little upset about your telling Jimmy Galton you saw him," Jewel said amiably. "But he knows you had to do it; why the hell wouldn't you? Course, he was out to my place, not riding his land.

Melba still ain't put two and two together—Martin and Leona, ha!—but she decided there was something fishy about Martin being out that morning. Up in the air she goes, stupid bitch! 'Martin,' I says, 'just ignore her.' When he comes home from church yesterday, she busts out crying and tells him now everybody's gonna know that he's cheatin' on her, how can she hold her head up, what about the kids (and them all grown), and so on and so forth."

Jewel's voice had risen in a whiny and accurate imitation of Melba Barnes. Now she resumed her normal robust tone. "But I told Martin that Catherine Linton, she was smarter than Melba, she might figure it out; though of course," and Jewel raised an emphatic eyebrow, "she wouldn't tell no one. 'She's a good girl,' I said, 'she's always kept her mouth shut tighter than a clam.'"

Jewel gave Catherine a firm nod of approval and dismissal, and Catherine silently replaced Tom's story on its spike and sidled out of the cubicle. She walked through the swinging door back into her own domain, knowing she had gotten a direct and forceful order to keep her nose out of Jewel's business.

Really, I think she overestimated me, Catherine thought with wry amusement as she rolled more paper into her typewriter. I don't think I ever would have thought of putting that particular "one and one" together. There's a woman with nerve. She makes me feel like I just graduated from diapers.

Then Catherine frowned and let her fingers rest idle on the keys. Would Martin Barnes have paid blackmail to keep his affair with Jewel a secret? Jewel would have said, in effect, "Publish and be damned," but Martin Barnes was a different kettle of fish. Based on her limited knowledge of Melba Barnes, Catherine decided that if Melba had good grounds for divorce, she would take Martin for whatever she could get. And that would be a considerable sum.

Maybe Martin had gotten sick of blackmail. The pressure of trying to have a surreptitious affair in little Lowfield, added to a bad relationship with a jealous wife, might have tipped Martin's scales toward violence; especially with the additional squeeze of having to pay hush money.

Sheriff Galton hadn't mentioned how much cash he had found in Leona's house. Had it all been blackmail money? How many people in Lowfield had secrets they would pay to keep hidden?

A week ago Catherine would have said, "Not many." But yesterday Tom had told her about Jimmy Galton Junior's drug sales. Today Jewel Crenna had told her she was having an affair with a prominent planter.

How many more people had mud tracking up their homes? And Sheriff Galton had hinted strongly at some other illegal activity the former nurse had engaged in.

It's a comment on how I felt about Leona, that I can accept the fact that she was a blackmailer, without being awfully surprised, Catherine reflected.

The swinging door rocked back and forth as Salton Sims, the *Gazette*'s press operator, came through. Salton approached everything at an angle, so until the moment he ended up at the side of her desk, Catherine had hopes she would be bypassed. Salton had appeared to be heading toward the filing cabinets.

"I missed seeing you when you was in the back," he said cheerfully.

Catherine's heart sank. No escape. Salton was known and dreaded throughout the county for his complete tactlessness and his equally complete determination to have his say.

"Bet that ole Leona Gaites was a sight with her head bashed in," Salton began. "Bloody, huh?"

Catherine cast around for help, but Tom was still away at the courthouse.

"Yes, Salton, she sure was, and I'd just as soon not discuss it, if you don't mind," Catherine said hopefully.

Salton stuck his hands in the pockets of his grease-soaked jump suit and grinned at Catherine.

"Well, you know what I say?" he asked her.

"I'll bet you're going to tell me."

"Damn right! No one can call me two-faced."

Boy, that's the truth, she thought.

"I say," he continued, "that it's a good thing."

"Salton!" She shouldn't have been shocked, but she was. Out of the corner of her eye, she saw Leila come into the room and begin filing at the bank of cabinets. Maybe Leila's presence would inhibit Salton, who thought all females under twenty were sacred. But no such luck.

"No, Catherine, you just think about it. It was a good thing. Leona was a godless woman."

"Godless?" repeated Catherine weakly. How long has it been since I heard anyone called that? She wondered. Only Salton would use that adjective.

"Sure, sure. I know for a fact, from a lady I won't name, that she killed babies."

Catherine finally understood what Leona had used some of Dr. Linton's equipment for. She glanced at Leila desperately and saw that Leila was shaken to the bone, staring in horror at Salton's broad face.

"I guess you mean that she performed abortions," Catherine said slowly.

"That's what a lady told me," Salton said with satisfaction.

"But they're legal," Catherine protested. "You can get them thirty miles away in Memphis." Were they legal in Mississippi? She couldn't remember.

"Too many people from here go to Memphis every day," Salton rebutted. "Any kid from here who went to Memphis for a thing like that would be caught in a minute. And what teenager could leave here for two days to go to Jackson, without their parents finding out what for and why?"

"True," Catherine admitted.

"Well, back to that cursed old press," Salton said happily, and wandered swiftly through the door, by some trick appearing until the last minute to be on a collision course with the wall.

Abortions. Wonderful. Abortion and blackmail payments: what a legacy I've inherited! That's where those medical instruments went: Leona was supplementing her Social Security.

Catherine caught herself bundling all her hair together and holding it on top of her head, a nervous habit she thought she had discarded with college exams. But she remained like that, both elbows out in the air, until she caught sight of Leila, whom she had completely forgotten.

Leila seemed equally oblivious of Catherine. She was still looking at the swinging door through which Salton had passed, her face so miserable that Catherine felt obliged to ask her if she was feeling sick.

"Listen," said Leila urgently, then stopped to look back through the archway that led into the reception area. There was no one there, but Leila came and sat close to Catherine's desk. The girl was still clutching a handful of bills she had been filing.

"Listen," she said again, and hunched over until her face was five inches from Catherine's. Catherine had to resist an urge to lean back.

"I'm listening," Catherine said sharply. She had an ominous feeling she was about to hear yet another secret.

"She *did*," Leila hissed dramatically.

"Perform abortions?"

"Yeah, sure," Leila whispered. "Listen, I know you won't tell on me . . ."

Everyone certainly seems to be sure of *that*, Catherine thought fleetingly.

". . . . but she 'did' me. It's like Mr. Sims says, how could I just tell my parents I was going to be out of town for two days?"

"When was this?"

"Five months ago."

After Father died, Catherine realized with relief. Leona just kept some of the equipment when Jerry bought the rest. At least it wasn't while her Father was alive.

"I went up to Memphis and asked, but it was awful expensive."

"Leona was cheap?"

"Oh, yeah, compared to Memphis. But I think she charged more later. I was one of her first."

Catherine felt sick.

"I'm sorry, Leila." It was all she knew to say.

"Oh, well." Leila waved a polished hand to dismiss her former predicament. "What I'm scared of," she went on urgently, "is the sheriff will tell, if he finds out. My parents, you know. I mean, what if Miss Gaites kept records?"

"Come on, Leila," Catherine said tartly. "She would hardly have a receipt file!"

Leila pondered that.

"I guess you're right," she said. "I mean, she was

breaking the law. So she probably wouldn't have written anything down. And you had to pay her cash."

Catherine imagined Leila trying to write a check for Leona's services and winced.

Leila, now that her immediate fear was banished, looked brighter by the second. She straightened her shoulders, leaned back in her chair, and gave her pink fingernails a once-over. Catherine was glancing at her notes surreptitiously, longing to return to something normal and humdrum, when the girl began to frown.

"How did you know about Tom's fiancée?" Leila asked abruptly.

"What?" Catherine made herself pay attention.

"Tom," Leila prompted. "When did he tell you?"

"That they broke up?" Catherine made an effort to remember. "I guess it was yesterday."

"He over at your place?" asked Leila, with badly feigned indifference.

"Oh," Catherine said, enlightened. "No, I went over to his house" (that just made it worse, she saw instantly) "and he happened to mention it in the course of the conversation."

And I was trying to do her a good turn, Catherine reflected gloomily, as Leila shot her a look and rose from her chair. Leila returned to her filing, back pointedly stiff, slamming home the drawers of the cabinets with all her strength.

It seemed a good time to go to lunch.

9

CATHERINE SPENT THE afternoon dodging con-
versations. She didn't want to hear any more
secrets or opinions.

The entire staff was aware of her penchant for long
silences, and when she gave minimal answers to direct questions she couldn't avoid, they got the point.

Finally Catherine caught up with her work. She had
deposited with Jewel everything urgent she had pending, with the nagging exception of the Barnes's grandchild's birthday-party piece.

She had seen a couple of stories by Randall on the
"set" spike when she carried her own things back. In

addition to turning out editorials, Randall had to report the occasional event, when Catherine and Tom were too busy to cover it. The *Gazette* simply couldn't afford another reporter, even though another pair of hands at a typewriter would often have been welcome, particularly in the fall when high school sports started up.

Catherine remembered the time she had had to cover a basketball game, during the hiatus between Tom's predecessor's departure and Tom's arrival. It had been a fiasco, and she shuddered to recall it, even months later.

Mrs. Weilenmann, the head librarian, came in to give Catherine the schedule for the next month's special library programs. Catherine thanked her wholeheartedly for the neatly typed listing. (All too often, people brought in scrawls that Catherine had to type up to decipher.) In a gush of gratitude, she promised to place it prominently in the next issue, with a border around it.

"Catherine," the tall middle-aged woman said slowly, after she had gathered up her paraphernalia to leave, "I'm worried about you and your situation."

Catherine stared blankly at Mrs. Weilenmann's toffee-colored face. Mrs. Weilenmann was intelligent, ugly, and charming; and Catherine had grown fond of her. But they had never had a really personal conversation.

"It occurred to me this morning," Mrs. Weilenmann said hesitantly, "when I was getting the books out of the bookdrop (and someone's hit it again; why can't people control their cars?)—well, it occurred to me that you are a little isolated now."

Catherine couldn't think of anything to say, so she waited.

"Not—socially; I don't know about that. But geographically."

"Oh?" murmured Catherine, mystified.

"Well, dear, I don't mean to make you nervous," Mrs. Weilenmann said in her peculiarly formal diction, "but the Drummonds are gone, aren't they? Having a great time, I hear, but they won't be back for a couple of weeks. And the library is closed at night, in the summer, after six on weekdays; and for most of the weekend. So to one side of you and across from you, there's no one. And on the other side of you, the street. But no one can see your yard from the street, because of the hedge. And behind you, there's the hedge again, so the other reporter (he still rents from you, doesn't he?) can't see your back yard. And being single, I imagine Mr. Mascalco isn't there often. At night."

Catherine gathered her hair up in a bundle and held it on top of her head.

"I don't mean to frighten you. I guess this sounds like I'm trying to. Really, I think I shouldn't have said anything. But I hate to think of you alone in your house at night. Now I'm sorry I started this," she finished in a distressed rush.

"What all this was leading up to (now that I've made a fool of myself by scaring you out of your wits) is that if you would like to stay with me, until this incident gets cleared up, I would love to have you."

And in Lowfield that was, though Catherine could never compliment her for it, a remarkably brave offer from a black woman to a white woman. Not only was Mrs. Weilenmann risking a shocked refusal, but, if Catherine accepted, Mrs. Weilenmann would be extremely cramped in her rented crackerbox of a house—which was situated, like Bethesda Weilenmann, in a gray area between the black and white parts of town.

"It sure is kind of you to offer," Catherine said slowly. "I really appreciate it. But I think I won't take you up on that, unless I get scared." That seemed inadequate, and Catherine groped around for another way to explain.

"You like being on your own," Mrs. Weilenmann

said unexpectedly and accurately. "I can understand; I do too. It isn't easy for me to be 'company' even overnight. I like to leave and go back to my own place, such as it is." Her face turned up in a smile. "So I do understand. But if you reconsider, I have a cot I can set up, and it would be no trouble at all. You're a brave young woman, Catherine. And you're not stupid, not stupid at all."

Catherine thought sadly that Mrs. Weilenmann must have been very disappointed in many people, to be so firm in praising these paltry recommendations.

"Thanks for your good opinion," Catherine said, and gave Mrs. Weilenmann one of her own rare smiles.

"I'll see you, then," Mrs. Weilenmann said briskly, and headed back to her library.

Mrs. Weilenmann's article would have an extra-thick border, Catherine resolved.

It had been a long day, even for a Monday. Catherine was covering her typewriter with a definite sense of relief as Tom walked in.

"I haven't seen you since this morning," she said idly. "Have you been working on the story about Leona?"

"Yeah," Tom replied, one hand on the door. "I took my basic story back to Jewel this morning, but I told her to expect additions. I've interviewed everyone who knows anything, and I haven't come up with a damn thing more than I knew this morning."

"You've been doing that all day?"

"No. I went to the Lion's Club meeting, too, for their usual ham and potato salad fest and speeches. The lieutenant governor spoke today. And then I had trouble with my car. I'll have to take it into the shop again now."

"Too bad," Catherine said politely. "See you to-morrow."

She began walking to her car, which was parked across the street by the courthouse.

"Catherine!"

She turned and saw Randall hurrying across the street after her.

As she watched him come toward her, she realized she had been too busy all day to think about the date he had made with her that morning.

"How was today?" he asked.

"If you really want to know—" she said, and laughed.

"Salton been asking too many graphic questions?"

"Salton," said Catherine, shaking her head. "Salton says, and I have it from another source, that Leona was an abortionist. That explains something Sheriff Galton said to me yesterday."

"Good God," Randall said mildly. "I had no idea we had a village abortionist." He brooded for a moment. "What did Galton say yesterday?" he asked finally, frowning.

"He asked if I sold to Leona, or knew she had, some things from Father's office. A sterilizer and instruments, I suppose, from what she seems to have been doing to support herself in her retirement." Catherine's voice was arid.

"He thinks you knew? Aided and abetted?"

"Yes. Or alternatively, that I was a customer."

Randall touched her hand.

"Oh well. I can't convince him different," she said. "*And* that's not all."

"More? You *have* had a busy day."

"I'll tell you now. We didn't talk about this yesterday," Catherine said, putting her purse on the car hood and leaning against the driver's door. He settled companionably beside her.

"Leona left her money, her house, the whole kit and kaboodle, to my father. Naturally, she had made this will before he died, and just never changed it. I wish to God she had."

"You're the legatee now?"

"So it seems. Sheriff Gallon apparently thinks that constitutes a motive for me . . . and I guess it would, at that, if I didn't have some money of my own. I like money," she said simply, "but I'm not avid for more." She paused to return the wave of Mrs. Brighton, the mayor's secretary.

"But to keep to the track—Sheriff Galton didn't give me a figure, but it seems there was quite a lot of money stashed in that little house. Now, I can't imagine that many girls in Lowfield needed abortions. I think the bulk of it has to be blackmail payments."

Randall nodded thoughtfully. She wanted to touch his hair.

"I have evidently been living in a dream," Catherine went on quietly, "because I am really—flabbergasted—that so many people in Lowfield were blackmailable, if that's a word."

"Who? Did Galton name names?" asked Randall, looking at the ground.

Catherine was sharply reminded that Randall was a newspaper editor, in the business of spreading information. She became acutely uneasy at the way he was carefully avoiding her eyes. It was a moment of testing; she saw that painfully. Maybe I am brave, like Mrs. Weilenmann said, she thought bleakly. She had opened her mouth to speak, when a new line of thought occurred to her. She asked, "Randall? Not you? Blackmail?"

He looked sad behind his glasses. He knew as well as she that this was a test of faith that had come too early; she could see that in his face.

He took a deep breath. "Not me," he said. "Maybe my mother."

Catherine had tensed, afraid that they were going to shatter their fragile beginning. Now she relaxed.

"Miss Angel?" she said, incredulously. "I thought she was made of iron."

"She is," he answered with a half-smile. "But she has her chink. My father. He was a famous man, Catherine, at least in this state, and the newspaper is such a family tradition. Even a little weekly newspaper can become a name, when people like my grandfather and father run it. They were crusaders in their way. Brilliant men. Men who always had enemies.

"And my father, I've found out, once took a bribe."

"You don't have to tell me," she said swiftly, dismayed.

"Well, just the outline." He took a moment to

frame what he wanted to say. "The paper was losing money. Crusaders lose advertising revenue. Even though this is the only paper in the county, some people would rather rely on word-of-mouth, or advertising in the Memphis papers that everyone here takes, than pay money to the *Gazette*; at least while Dad was running it. And you know our family money was tied up by my great-grandfather; we can't pump it into the *Gazette*. So at a critical point my father accepted some money from someone running for office, to keep the paper going. The candidate didn't want one of his activities made known. My father was the only newspaperman who knew of this— activity." Randall pulled off his glasses and rubbed his eyes.

Catherine was trying to hide her shock Randall's father had been one of her heroes.

"My mother found out after he died, when she went through his personal papers. I reckon she thought she had hidden all the traces, but I found them when I took over the paper, and I asked her about it. She told me, finally. And I know she would give anything to have no one else on earth know."

Catherine felt honored that Randall had shown confidence in her.

"I don't think you should worry," she said gently.

"I don't see how Leona could have known—unless your father told mine at his office, where she could have heard."

"It's possible. They were friends. Close friends."

"You've been brooding about this."

"Not yesterday," he said, with the ghost of a smile. "But today, yes, I have. I heard rumors Saturday night, about Leona's—sideline. One of the deputies couldn't keep his mouth shut about the blackmail material and money they found in Leona's house. Or maybe Galton wanted that leaked, to stir things up and see what rose to the surface."

"Miss Angel," Catherine began, and faltered. "You know your mother better than anyone else, I'm sure. But from what I know of Miss Angel, I'd just out-and-out ask her if she had been paying Leona to keep quiet. Your mother's that kind of woman. I think if she'd wanted to do away with Leona, she would've shot her on the courthouse steps at high noon."

"I think so too," Randall said, and grinned at her. "Now that I've spilled my guts, what about yours?"

With no hesitation, she told him about Jewel Crenna and Martin Barnes, and about Sheriff Galton's son.

Randall whistled.

"Sounds like the entire population of Lowfield

might have had excellent reasons to want Leona dead."

"I know," Catherine said. "I was so positive that the reason Leona died was the same reason my parents died. Now, I'm not sure."

"Does it eat at you? Your parents?"

"How could it not? Vengeance sounds melodramatic. the very word . . . but that's what I want. I want vengeance." She stopped. "This may not be what you want a woman to say to you, or what you want a woman to be." She clenched her fists and tried to pick her words with absolute accuracy. "But at my core, where I really live, I want vengeance on whoever killed my parents. My mother and father should not have died like that. It has altered me."

"I would wonder," he said quietly, "only if you didn't feel that way."

They stirred, shaking off the grip of strong emotions, ready to turn to light things, normal subjects.

"Pick out a movie you want to see Friday," Randall said.

"Early showing or late?"

"Late. We'll have dinner first, if that suits you."

He opened her car door with an exaggerated flourish.

"I declare, sir, how kind of you," Catherine said with an extravagant drawl and a simper.

Randall choked a surprised laugh.

"I am your servant, you sweet flower of Southern womanhood," he responded instantly.

She gripped his hand for a second and then started the engine. She watched him walk back into the office before she pulled out to go home.

It was a lackluster evening. Catherine found herself wandering around the house in search of something to do.

I'm completely shaken out of pattern, she reflected. And a good thing, too. Not much of a pattern to stick to.

There was dust on the furniture, and the bathroom needed a thorough scrubbing. This lack of order made Catherine irritable, but she was too restless to begin clearing it up.

When she started putting the clean dishes back into the kitchen cabinets, she came to a stop as her hand fell on an unfamiliar shape. Mrs. Perkins's casserole dish. Returning it was something concrete and necessary. She marched out her front door in a glow of virtue.

I'll thank her so nicely and be such a lady she won't be able to say a word about me. Catherine resolved.

The long summer day was fading as she left her house. She stopped on her doorstep to drink in the evening. The sky in the west was stained a dark strawberry-juice pink. The locusts were in full voice, their drone rising and falling in hypnotic rhythm. The humid warmth made her skirt limp against her legs, but the air was no longer stifling. As she moved on with a slower step, the grass rustled around her feet.

The streetlights were on. Catherine emerged from her yard onto the silent street, passing under the lamp at the corner. As she crossed the pavement, she barely bothered to glance right and left. It was a time for quiet in Lowfield.

She was embraced by the dusk, cast back for a few minutes into the time before Saturday, when she had felt shielded by the safety of her own town, street, and house, her unassailable heritage of land and good family.

Catherine sighed as she walked up the gleaming white concrete to the Perkins's pillared verandah. As she lifted the polished brass knocker, she returned to the present.

It was a signal of her intention to be formal that

she went to the front door, instead of to the back as a good neighbor would.

Carl Perkins answered the door. Catherine had been expecting Miss Molly, for some reason, and for a moment she was startled as his thickened frame filled the doorway. She wondered how he could endure the long sleeves he always wore. As a gust of air from the house rushed out to meet her, she decided she understood his preference, at least in his own home. The air was not only cooled, it was refrigerated.

"Catherine Linton! Come on in," he said, with no trace of surprise, only welcome.

He ushered her through the two-story entrance hall and into the living room. Miss Molly, dwarfed in the corner of an enormous beige couch, rose as Catherine entered. The little woman had some knitting in her hand, and she carefully set it down before she advanced to greet Catherine.

"I enjoyed the gumbo so much," Catherine said, smiling her most correct smile and extending the casserole dish to Miss Molly, who looked mildly flustered.

"So glad you enjoyed it, just some leftovers really," Molly Perkins deprecated properly. She took the proferred dish and went full tilt toward the back of the house, where, Catherine remembered, the enormous kitchen lay.

"Bring our neighbor some coffee," Mr. Perkins called after the dumpy retreating figure.

Catherine raised a hand in protest, but it was too late.

"Come on, have a seat. Been a while since we got to visit with you," Mr. Perkins urged.

She thought he was lonely. She managed another smile and sat reluctantly in a deep armchair facing the couch. As she sank farther and farther into it, she wondered how she was going to get up with any grace, with her short legs thrust out at such an angle.

Miss Molly came back in, burdened with a tray. Mr. Perkins was on his feet in an instant.

"You shouldn't carry things like that," he chided. "Why didn't you call me?"

"I can carry this perfectly well, I'm not made of glass," she scolded him.

Mr. Perkins peered over Miss Molly's curly gray hair to give Catherine a wry shake of the head.

"How do you take yours, Catherine?" Miss Molly asked as she settled back on the couch.

"Black, please," Catherine answered. "I hope this wasn't any trouble for you."

"No, no," disclaimed Carl Perkins. "We always have a pot on at night until we go to bed.

"I saw you through the window at the *Gazette*

today," he resumed, as Miss Molly poured, "and I started to come in and speak, but you looked so busy I thought the better of it."

"Mondays are mighty busy at the paper," Catherine responded. She disliked being reminded of how "on view" she was, with her desk right by the big window. It had bothered her when she first began working at the *Gazette*, but now she wasn't conscious of it most of the time.

Miss Molly handed Catherine her cup. A lot of wriggling was required before Catherine could work herself forward in her chair to reach it. Miss Molly's hand had a definite tremor, which didn't make the little transaction any easier.

Oh dear oh damn, Catherine thought. She wished she had just handed over the dish and gone right back out the door. Her intention of impressing Miss Molly with her sterling character and imperviousness to gossip seemed childish now.

Carl Perkins had just started to comment on the effect the rainless summer was having on the cotton when Molly Perkins's shaky hands caused an incident. His attention on Catherine, Mr. Perkins held out a hand for his coffee cup. When Molly extended the cup to him, some of the steaming liquid spilled on his hand. For a long moment, as Catherine held her breath in sympathy for his pain, he kept his eyes on her face as if he felt nothing. Then Mrs. Perkins's eyes teared as if she were going to cry over her mistake.

"Oh, Carl!" she said in a trembling, guilty voice. He looked at her, then down at the coffee that had run off his hand and stained the beautiful beige material of the couch.

Mrs. Perkins somehow kept hold of the cup, rescuing it before it spilled completely. Then there was the fuss of Mr. Perkins's retreat to the bathroom to put cold water and ointment on his burned hand, Mrs. Perkins's agonized exclamations, and Catherine's attempt to leave, which was firmly crushed by Mr. Perkins as he marched off to the bathroom.

As all this was being settled, Catherine passed from being uncomfortable to being miserable. She obviously disturbed Miss Molly for some reason; and she had no business sitting around frightening an old lady into burning her husband and staining expensive upholstery. But to extricate herself from this little visit without being out-and-out rude would have required more dexterity than Catherine could muster at the moment.

The scene jelled again as Mr. Perkins entered and sat down as though nothing had happened, quieting his wife's attempt at yet another apology with a soothing, "Now don't fuss any more, honey." Mr. Perkins was stoically controlling the pain he must have felt from the burn.

How kind he is to act as if it doesn't even hurt, Catherine thought. They must have a good marriage. They've come a long way together.

After Carl Perkins had come to Lowfield from Louisiana, he had climbed in the town and bought a business; then climbed more and bought more, with Miss Molly joining clubs right and left, working in the church, entertaining. The Perkins's only child was their son Josh. There were mementos of Josh everywhere: football trophies, baseball trophies, 4-H medals, and framed certificates. Catherine hadn't seen Josh in years. She recalled him as arrogant and insensitive, but intelligent in a graceless way. He had been one of Lowfield High School's golden boys.

Now he was married, about to become a father; and far, far away from Lowfield, Mississippi. Los Angeles, hadn't Miss Molly said?

Catherine was craftily preparing a lead-in to the subject of Josh, aware that little would be required of her if she could get Mr. Perkins launched, when Mr. Perkins himself jumped the conversational gun.

"I went to the Lion's Club meeting today," he observed. "Sure am glad I'm not running that outfit anymore. It's nice to take a back seat and let somebody else do the work."

But you have to mention that you *were* the president, Catherine commented silently. She remembered that after the inaugural party for the Perkins mansion, her mother had said with despair, "Self-made men are the proudest men on earth!"

"How was the lieutenant governor's speech?" asked Catherine brightly.

"He's campaigning now, so it was pretty agreeable," Mr. Perkins replied, smiling.

"What did he have to say?" Catherine murmured, relieved to have found such an innocuous topic.

"If he had had a lot to say, he wouldn't be lieutenant governor!" answered Mr. Perkins cheerfully.

Catherine laughed without much effort. Mrs. Perkins gave the tolerant smile of someone who had heard the same remark before.

The older woman had finally relaxed. She picked up her knitting and began to work on it expertly. Catherine saw that it was something tiny.

"For your grandchild?" she asked.

"Yes," Miss Molly admitted with a proud smile.

"Josh and his wife say it'll be here in December,"

said Mr. Perkins eagerly, and Catherine had only to smile and nod for the next ten minutes.

"Of course, I had counted on Josh living here with us," he wound down. "Now Molly and me are just rattling around in this big house like peas in a hollow pod. I got all these businesses here, and no one to run 'em after I'm gone."

Catherine felt sorry for the aging man, who had come to Lowfield practically penniless, her father had told her. Now there was no one to share the comfort of the easy years. The dynasty he had wanted to found had taken off for the golden coast.

Catherine rose awkwardly and evaded the obligatory urgings to stay, have more coffee, talk longer.

On her way out, she passed a bank of photographs on a wall. She stopped to comment on a wedding portrait of Josh's wife, whom she had never met.

"Very fine family," Carl Perkins said with satisfaction. "Been in Natchez forever."

After Catherine agreed that "Josh's wife" was lovely (what is the girl's name, Catherine wondered, or do they just call her "J.W."?), she was obliged to look at the rest of the pictures. Josh at all ages, in all varieties of sports uniform; Mrs. Perkins with a prize-winning flower arrangement; Mr. Perkins being sworn in to several offices.

One of the pictures had a duplicate in the files at the *Gazette*. Whatever past reporter had snapped it must have presented Mr. Perkins with an enlargement. In the framed copy before her, Catherine saw him breaking ground for a new store. Heavy dark brows gave his rough face distinction, and upright shoulders lent an impression of vigor.

She looked at the man beside her now, and for a moment the hand of time lay heavy on her shoulder. Carl Perkins's skin had a curious patched look, his hair was thinning, and his eyebrows were almost non-existent. His sleeve, rolled up for the bandage over the burn, revealed an arm marked by irregular dark spots. This pleasant, hearty, proud man was going, bit by bit.

Miss Molly, in her own yellowed wedding portrait before Catherine on the wall, was small and smiling in her old-fashioned veil. Now her face was tracked with fine wrinkles. Instead of a wedding bouquet, she was clutching a bundle of knitting intended for a grandchild.

For a rotten moment, Catherine thought of the single gray hair she had pulled from her own dark head that morning, and remembered the tiny lines she had spotted at the corners of her eyes. She thought of Leona Gaites, grimly independent and dignified, performing cheap abortions in her little house and listening carefully for other peoples' cheap secrets, in order to finance an old age that would never come.

Then the room, gracious and overdone, came into focus again, and Carl and Molly Perkins were a kind couple with many years left to them—years that promised the pleasure of seeing in babies' faces traces of their own genes.

"Now you take care of yourself," said Mr. Perkins with a smile. "Don't you go getting into any more trouble. Remember, we're always here when you need us."

In the face of his kindness and concern, Catherine felt a sharp pang because of the fun she had poked at his ostentatious house. Her goodbyes were guiltily warm. Mr. Perkins offered to walk her home.

Catherine said, "It's just a few feet. No need to go to all that trouble."

"Honey," said Mr. Perkins with sudden gravity, "you, of all people, should know that things aren't safe around here."

Without waiting for an answer, he stepped out onto the verandah.

It was fully dark now. No strawberry-juice stains in the sky, but blue darkness. The moon was full. The locusts were still chorusing throughout the quiet town. The streetlight at the corner of Catherine's lot seemed brighter against the full night.

And suddenly she was glad for the firm feet of Carl Perkins walking beside her, for the easy commonplace observation he was making about the need to repave Linton Street.

Then he said abruptly, "You'll have to excuse Molly, Catherine. I know you noticed how shaky she is."

"Is she ill?" Catherine asked gently. He doesn't need to explain, she thought. Miss Molly believes I killed Leona, somehow. And she's scared of me.

"No, she's just plain scared."

That fit in so neatly with her thoughts that Catherine stopped to stare at Mr. Perkins. Was he going to tell her to her face that Miss Molly feared her?

Mr. Perkins was waiting for Catherine to say, "Of what?" When she didn't, he stopped too, and looked back at her.

"Why," he said, just as if she had supplied the expected words, "she's scared for you."

"*For* me?" Catherine asked cautiously. That preposition made a world of difference.

"Well, sure, honey. After all . . ." and here self-assured Carl Perkins floundered. "I mean . . . several people close to you have . . ."

148

"Been murdered," Catherine said impassively. I don't know but what I'd rather be a suspected killer than a potential victim, she reflected.

"Yes," said Mr. Perkins, as if the sad truth had to be admitted at last. "If you knew why they died, it might be mighty dangerous for you."

"I wish I knew," she said slowly. "Sheriff Galton said he thought the motives were separate." She had no desire to talk about what the sheriff had found in Leona's house. Leona had been a blackmailer, an abortionist, and Catherine knew her father had been none of those things. She didn't think anyone who had known him would suspect for one minute that he had been involved in Leona's evil. No, Leona's brief life of crime had started after Dr. Linton's death; and it was for one of those crimes, surely, that Leona had been killed. So the murders must not be related. That was James Galton's line of reasoning.

And I was halfway convinced of it too, Catherine thought. But the sheriff is wrong. I know he's wrong.

"I wish I knew," she repeated, looking up at Mr. Perkins under the streetlight.

He looked unutterably sad. "I know you miss your folks," he murmured, and touched her shoulder.

They began moving slowly through Catherine's yard.

"I hate like hell," he continued, "that Molly and I weren't able to be at the funeral."

Stop, Catherine begged him silently. Even now, she couldn't endure her memory of that gray day.

"We tried to change our reservations, but it was so close to Christmas that it was just impossible," he said.

"You went to see Josh out in California?" Catherine asked, trying to move him off the subject.

"Yes. Our plans had been made for so long; the airlines couldn't find other flights . . . it was just hopeless. I wish I had been here to help you settle your daddy's affairs," he said with regret in his voice. "But by the time we got back, Jerry Selforth had gotten himself all set up. Goddamn, Catherine, I'm sorry about your folks!"

The loss wasn't just mine, Catherine reflected for the hundredth time. It was everyone's.

They mounted Catherine's front steps.

"Thanks for walking me home."

"Sure, my pleasure," he said heartily. "Want me to come in and check the house for you?"

"Oh, I don't think you need to do that." She had locked the front door behind her when she left, for the first time in her life worried about leaving it open for a brief period. She unlocked it now, and glanced in at the living room. "See, all clear!" She attempted lightness.

"Okay," said Mr. Perkins, satisfied after scanning the undisturbed room.

"Goodbye now," Catherine said. She stepped inside the house.

"Oh, heck."

Catherine turned back.

"I been meaning to ask you ever since Christmas. Josh wants his medical records. Does Jerry Selforth have everything of your daddy's?"

Damn Josh, she thought vehemently. He's got them wrapped around his finger for life.

This was a confirmation of the train of thought Randall had started in her head Sunday afternoon. In almost the same breath, even Carl Perkins could regret her parents' eternal absence and then move on to his son's record of vaccinations and measles.

"No," she replied, suddenly exhausted and sick. "It's probably up in the attic at the old office, since there's been no call for it since Father died. I'll get it for you."

"No, no, don't worry about it now, Catherine." Perkins seemed to realize the wound he had given. "There's no hurry in the world."

"Okay. I'll get it in a couple of days, maybe."

He started down the walkway after clumsily patting her shoulder again with his bandaged hand.

She called goodbye after him. Her voice hung
heavy in the living humid warmth of the night air.

☀

Mrs. Weilenmann had pointed out Catherine's isolation. Carl Perkins had pointed out that three people
connected with her were dead. Despite her refusal of
Mr. Perkins's offer, she went through every room in
the house before she went to bed.

"Thanks a lot, folks," she muttered, as she locked
herself inside her bedroom.

10

THE MULTITUDE OF Monday's revelations had worn Catherine down. She slept heavily, despite the Perkins's coffee, and woke groggy.

Tuesday, like Monday, began off-center. She overslept by ten minutes, an irritating breach of her workday morning routine. To make up the time, she had to scramble into her clothes while the coffee was perking, and skip a cup of that coffee. She promised herself to make up for it at the office, from the big urn kept continuously filled in the production room.

The telephone rang while she was making her bed. She was back on schedule and in a better humor, so instead of assuming that the call would be dire news, she predicted some mild disturbance, which was what it proved to be.

"My damn car's in the shop," Tom said without preamble. "Can you give me a ride to work?"

"Sure, come on over," Catherine replied promptly.

This had happened before. Tom's ancient Volkswagen, noisy and battle-scarred, was subject to drastic breakdowns and expensive repairs.

Catherine was at the back door to let him in when he knocked.

"I was just about ready to leave, I'm glad you caught me," she said, checking her purse to make sure she had her keys.

"No telling how much it's going to cost this time," Tom said gloomily. "I took it over to Don's Garage after work yesterday, and he said he'd bring it by this morning. Said it was nothing hard to fix, he could do it in a couple of hours."

"That's what Don always says," Catherine told him.

"Why?" asked Tom, outraged. "If he had just told me he'd have to keep it, I could have called you last night."

"He just likes people to leave happy," Catherine said. "That's the way Don is. I'm surprised you hadn't caught on to that by now, as much trouble as you've had with that car.

"At least," she added as they walked to her garage, "it'll be fixed when you *do* get it back."

"I have plans for tonight, so he better get his ass in gear." Tom said, folding himself into Catherine's front seat. She wondered, not for the first time, how he managed in the Volkswagen.

"I doubt he will," Catherine warned.

Tom sulked all the way to the office. That was fine with Catherine, who didn't feel like idle chatter before nine o'clock at the earliest.

Leila was looking out the front window when Catherine pulled into a parking space miraculously open in front of the *Gazette* office. Usually the court-house people took all the good spots, arriving early to stake their claims. Her little triumph dissolved into a flat feeling when she saw Leila's face become woebe-gone at the sight of the two of them arriving together.

By the time Catherine and Tom came in through the glass door that had "Lowfield Gazette" stenciled across it in gothic lettering, Leila was sitting rigidly erect at her typewriter behind the counter, pounding the keys furiously.

What a temper she's got, Catherine thought, pass-ing through the little reception room without a word. She wanted to go up to Leila and shake her by the shoulders.

She realized belatedly that Tom had not followed her into the reporters' room. She heard the whisper of voices behind her. It looked as if Tom and Leila were getting together. Maybe Leila was Tom's "plans for the evening."

Catherine made a wry face at her typewriter and then shrugged. The paper would go to press that afternoon, and would be delivered the next morning. There was a lot to do before the noon deadline.

She began checking over what she had written the day before. Jewel had left the proofs on her desk. Catherine had to proofread all her own stories, then pass them back to Production to be reread by Sarah, the paste-up girl, before she placed them on the page. Catherine got out her felt-tipped pen and settled down to work. Tom came in after a moment with a smug look on his thin face.

The feathers are sticking out of your mouth, she told him silently, and then was distracted by a cathedral-length bridal "vail."

Almost to Catherine's surprise, and certainly to her relief, the morning passed as quietly as Tuesday mornings ever did at the *Gazette*. The usual last-minute crises came up, but Catherine was braced for them. A bride's picture was flipped, so her ring appeared on her right hand. Catherine caught that and set it to rights. The weekly Dr. Croft column was missing, and because of its great popularity with Lowfield subscribers, the search for it was a tense one. It was always pasted up days before the paper was due to come out, since it arrived set at the correct column width and had only to be cut off a sheet containing seven other Dr. Croft columns, each one headed with a line drawing of the handsome and fatherly doctor.

"Dr. Croft's Corner" had been unpopular with Catherine's father. Every time she read it, she recalled his indignation and impatience when two or three people came to his office after the appearance of each column, sure they had the disease Dr. Croft had expounded on that week.

Catherine wondered for a moment whether Jerry Selforth had the same problem.

At last sharp-eyed Jewel found the missing column. The wax holding it to the page had weakened, and the fan had blown it under the paste-up table. Catherine, with dirty hands and knees after taking an active part in the search, rose from the floor and repaired immediately to the *Gazette*'s rather dreadful ladies' room to clean up.

Leila, she noted sourly, had kept her own golden limbs pristine by promptly recalling some bills that had to be sent out, at the moment the column was discovered missing.

Tom was slumped at his desk when Catherine emerged from the ladies' room.

"I must have called the sheriff's office ten times," he complained, "and I always get the redneck queen, Mary Jane Cory. 'I'm sorry, Sheriff Galton is out. I'm sorry, Sheriff Galton is with someone right now.' I keep hearing all these rumors about Leona's past. and I want a quote from him on that!"

Catherine considered. She was a little pleased to know something Tom didn't know. She thought, He'd throttle me if he knew I was withholding a tidbit from him.

She almost told Tom to go ask Leila about the truth of what he had heard, but she knew she would never forgive herself if she did. As long as he had heard the rumors, though. She had a mischievous impulse.

"Go talk to Salton Sims," she said. pokerfaced. "Salton knows something."

"If I voluntarily talk to Salton, I *must* be dedicated," Tom said grimly, and set out, with pad and pencil in hand, to locate the pressman.

Catherine almost laughed out loud. But her little moment of mischief promptly fizzled when she glanced down at her desk and saw a hole for a picture on her sketch of the society page. The space hadn't been crossed by the large "X" she drew whenever she sent a picture back to the offset darkroom.

"Omigod," she said guiltily. She had forgotten to call the Barnes house to remind them to deliver their grandchild's picture for today's paper. She had picked up the phone to dial, casting a quick glance at the clock on the wall as she did so (it was an hour from the deadline), when Martin Barnes himself came through the front door and into the reception area.

Catherine heard Leila directing him to the reporters' room—not that he needed much direction, since Catherine was in clear view—and then the planter was advancing across the worn carpet to stand before her desk. Catherine was self-conscious because of the conversation she had had with Jewel the day before. She examined Mr. Barnes covertly for signs of a romantic soul, but there he was: four-square Martin Barnes.

"How are you, Catherine?" he said mildly. "Haven't seen you to talk to in a coon's age."

Mr. Barnes's weathered but still handsome face expressed nothing but polite pleasure. Before Catherine could say anything, he went on. "I sure was surprised when Jimmy Gallon came out to my place yesterday. I didn't think it was so all-fired important that I was on the same road where Leona got dumped."

Catherine fluttered her hand in a meaningless gesture. She wished she hadn't sent Tom off on a wild-goose chase to interview Salton Sims. She had a second to think, That's what I get for being catty, before Barnes, slowly collecting his thoughts, began to ruminate again.

"I told him I was just out riding my land, same as I always do early in the morning," Barnes said, looking at Catherine significantly. "Well, little Catherine Linton saw me, Jimmy says, and right afterward she found something nasty, something mighty bad. Course, by then I had heard about old Leona Gaites at church, so it wasn't no surprise to me."

Catherine could think of no conceivable response. Her reputation for silence was serving her well, she decided, for Barnes didn't seem to expect a reply.

"And I said to him, 'Sure, I saw that gal.'" Barnes went on slowly. "I wondered at it, too, her being out so early on a Saturday morning. First time in my life the police ever come by my house to ask me questions. Parked in front of my house, for everyone to see." He sounded mildly resentful, but Catherine couldn't decide whether or not the resentment was aimed at her. "Melba 'bout went wild," he added glumly.

She wondered if Jewel had had time to report their conversation of yesterday to her lover.

"First time the police have ever been at my house, too," Catherine said, with a poor imitation of brightness. "And the last time, I hope."

From the corner of her eye, she saw Tom stalk into the room and cast a look of utter disgust in her direction. He threw his pad and pencil on his desk and walked directly out again. Catherine saw him lean on the counter in Leila's office, and heard the murmur of their voices.

No help from that quarter. Tom would happily let Martin Barnes talk her to death in retaliation for her sending him to Salton Sims to discover that Leona was "godless."

At least Barnes was smiling at her faint joke. He reached inside his pocket and drew out a photograph.

"Here's my picture of Chrissy for the paper," he explained carefully. "My first grandchild, you know." The planter beamed.

Catherine eyed the picture. It was even worse than the usual run of photos handed in to the *Gazette* for such celebrations. For one thing, it was in color, which reproduced poorly in the *Gazette*; Randall couldn't afford expensive color ink. For another thing, the little girl was slumped sideways in her highchair at practically a right angle, and her stare was woefully blank: no cute smile, no expression at all. Little Chrissy's goggle eyes and gape were ludicrous in combination with the gay party hat, with its crepe pompon that had unwisely been strapped to the child's head.

"Cute kid," said Catherine faintly.

"Looks just like her grandpa, Sally says."

That triggered laughter in Catherine, who decided that Martin was maligning himself. He was still a good-looking man, and this baby—Catherine bit the inside of her mouth ferociously, to keep from bursting into unforgivable giggles.

"Thanks for bringing it in," she managed, her voice only slightly choked. "I'll take it to the back right away, so it'll be in the paper when you get it tomorrow."

"We're looking forward to it," he assured her earnestly. "See you some other time, Catherine. I hope we don't meet out in the fields no more."

Catherine looked up from the picture sharply, but Barnes was already walking out. He had to turn sideways to edge through the reception room, for the little area had become crowded during their conversation.

Tom was still leaning over the counter talking to

Leila, Carl Perkins was standing nearby with a folder in his hands that must contain his enterprises' ads for the coming week, and, Catherine saw with a thud, Sheriff Galton was leaning against the wall with an air of infinite patience. Mrs. Weilenmann was standing with Randall in the doorway of his office, deep in discussion.

When Tom straightened up from the counter and turned to see who was behind him, his whole body stiffened (like a bird dog, Catherine thought), as he realized that the object of his phone calls was within reach. Catherine couldn't hear what he said, but she saw Galton shake his head, smiling, as Tom's mouth moved nonstop.

Tom went on talking, and Galton shook his head again, with less of a smile. Tom was being persistent. As usual, Mr. Perkins turned away, trying to appear uninvolved in their exchange. Randall and Mrs. Weilenmann finished their talk, and, as the librarian worked her way out of the knot of people, Randall ushered Galton into his office.

It was the first time she had seen Randall that day. He caught a glimpse of her face and gave her a quick wave.

Catherine smiled back. Mrs. Weilenmann, notic-
ing her at the same time, assumed the smile was for
her. She raised a hand in greeting.

As Catherine looked at the knot of familiar faces,
her smile suddenly stiffened. One of these, she thought.
Maybe one of these people . . . She saw an anonymous
arm rising and falling, saw blood pouring through gray
hair.

Why? she wondered frantically. Why? The nightmare was before her eyes again, all the more horrible
in this hot, sun-drenched, normal room. I'll face it,
she decided. I have to face it squarely.

She looked at the worst.

Randall, who had the strength of an athlete. His
reason: Leona's threats to expose his father's accep-
tance of a bribe. But, Catherine rebutted swiftly, he
told me about that himself, when he certainly didn't
need to. She then considered Randall's mother, Angel, for the same reason, but she knew Miss Angel
was not physically strong enough to kill someone in
the way Leona had been killed.

Sheriff Galton. His son was selling drugs. The
shame of it would break James Galton, privately and
publicly, if it became generally known. And Leona
had had a habit of finding things out.

Mrs. Weilenmann, that sad and misplaced woman.

Her rumored white husband was supposed to have been a lawyer. Why would such a woman return to the South, where she was neither fish nor fowl? Catherine had always imagined that a long sad story was buried behind those dignified toffee-colored features.

Tom had resumed his conversation with Leila. If Leona had seen Tom buying dope Friday night . . . A drug conviction would bar him from ever holding another reporting job. Reporters were too thick on the ground now for any editor to have to consider hiring a risk.

Leila? Catherine almost dismissed Leila offhand. But to be fair, she paused to consider her. After all, Leila had admittedly had criminal contact with Leona Gaites. But, like Randall, she seemed to be cleared by that very admission. Of course, Leila's father was a pillar of a fundamentalist church. I just don't know what Mr. Masham might do, if he knew his baby had gotten pregnant and had an abortion, Catherine thought.

And, of course, there were Martin Barnes and Jewel Crenna, the illicit couple.

This has gone far enough, Catherine told herself savagely, trying to arrange her face so it would have some semblance of normality for Mr. Perkins, who had dropped off his folder at Leila's desk and was coming toward her. I could add Carl and Molly Perkins, Salton Sims . . . Maybe I have blackouts and did it myself . . . Maybe the Drummonds aren't in Europe at all, but hiding out secretly in their house!

"Are you all right?"

Or none of the above, Catherine concluded before she looked up.

"Yes sir," she said. "I just had some bad thoughts."

"I guess we've all had them lately," Mr. Perkins said sadly. "Molly and I just wanted to know if you'd come over to supper at our house tonight. You can bring your boyfriend if you want to. Molly and I would sure like to get to know him better."

"Know him better?" Catherine was sure her jaw had gone slack with astonishment. What was this new kite of rumor sailing through the Lowfield sky?

"Your tenant," said Mr. Perkins with a trace of uncertainty in his voice. He bobbed his head backward in Tom's direction.

"He's just my tenant," Catherine said definitely. She smiled one of the killer smiles Southern women are taught. "I'm so sorry I won't be able to come over tonight. I'm way behind on everything I have to do at home."

"We're sure sorry you can't come," Mr. Perkins

said, flinching almost visibly, unable to apologize for fear of getting in deeper. "But if you get nervous about being on your lonesome, you just come right on over."

"Sure will," Catherine responded with absolute insincerity.

She watched her neighbor walk away. I guess I nipped that in the bud, she thought with some satisfaction.

The reception area had emptied while Catherine was talking with Mr. Perkins. She was glad. She wanted no more talk, no more suspicion. She wanted to work and be ignored. She quickly delivered baby Chrissy's picture to the darkroom, earning a glower from the camera operator because of its late arrival.

Leila was at her desk humming as she stapled statements to checks when Catherine passed through on her way to lunch. The girl looked almost elevated, as if she had received a call to a higher duty. Tom was evidently living up to his image in Leila's eyes. Catherine paused, wondering what Tom was going to do about lunch, since his car was in the shop; but she saw him through the plate-glass window crossing the courthouse lawn, headed toward the sandwich shop on the other side of the square. She supposed he was getting lunch for himself and Leila.

Catherine decided to go home rather than buy a sandwich. She would definitely be a third wheel.

As she drove, she tried to remember what the refrigerator contained that she could fix quickly.

The only raw ingredient around was lettuce. After eating a limp and unsatisfactory salad, Catherine was assembling a grocery list at the kitchen table when the telephone rang. As she reached up to answer it, she wondered who would be calling her at noon.

The voice that came over the line was so choked as to be almost unrecognizable.

"What are you doing with Martin, you little bitch? What do you mean, getting him into trouble?"

"Mrs. Barnes?" asked Catherine unbelievingly.

Her only answer was a few hiccuping sounds that could have been sobs.

My God, Catherine thought blankly.

"What are you talking about?" she ventured, into a silence so taut she imagined she could feel it vibrating. Melba Barnes, my fellow colorful Southern eccentric, Catherine thought wearily.

"I wanted to catch you at home, you little sneak, not down at the paper office where your little friend Tom Mascalco could listen in and laugh at me, too."

By now Catherine was recovering from her initial shock. Anger made her blood pump faster.

She had had enough.

Enough of Sheriff Galton's admonitions; enough of Jewel's hints about keeping her mouth shut, and Leila's nasty little confidences; enough mysterious half-threats from Martin Barnes; enough of the dark dealings of Leona Gaites.

In a careful low voice, she said, "I don't know what the hell you are implying, Mrs. Barnes. But I can tell you that I resent your tone and this entire conversation. Now if you have something to tell me, tell me and then shut up. Because if you ever repeat your suspicions to anyone else in this town, I will slap a lawsuit on you so fast your head will swim."

Another awful hiccup-sob.

"What were you and Martin doing in that shack, anyway? You told the police you saw him out there. I saw him in your office today, through that big window. I saw him talking to you. I knew then he had been lying about riding around the place. I've known for a long time he's been carrying on, but I never thought it would be with a girl his daughter's age!"

Catherine closed her eyes and leaned against the wall by the telephone. Yesterday, according to Jewel, Melba Barnes had suspected Leona; today, it was Catherine.

"I can't believe this," she said, unaware that she

had spoken out loud, until Mrs. Barnes gave a snort on the other end.

"Mrs. Barnes," Catherine said, in a voice so controlled and furious that she almost frightened herself, "I have no interest in your husband at all. I have never met him anywhere by prearrangement. I passed him by chance on a dirt road Saturday morning." Catherine had to resist a powerful temptation to tell her where her husband had been (Jewel should be the recipient of this blast, not me!). "When Sheriff Galton asked me if I had seen anyone, I told him I had seen Mr. Barnes. He was in his pickup and I was in my car. We were going in opposite directions. This morning he came by the office to give me your grandchild's picture to put in the newspaper. I think," Catherine ended heavily, "that you are crazy, and this whole conversation, if you can call it that, is disgusting." Then she hung the phone firmly on the wall.

The whole thing struck Catherine as being so sordid that she shook her fingers, as if to shake off the dirt transmitted by the telephone.

Catherine Linton, femme fatale, she thought wryly, when she had become a little calmer. Leila thought Tom and I were lovers; Carl Perkins, too. Now Mrs. Barnes thinks I've been screwing her dumb husband on the floor of a shack, with a dead woman beside us.

As she locked up the house, Catherine decided that today she didn't like anyone very much. She included herself in the group.

Leona's murder is like kicking over an anthill, she thought. Everyone is scurrying to get under new cover, treading over each other in their haste to escape exposure.

11

THE AFTERNOON WENT along quietly. The production staff was frantically busy getting the paper from the press and bundling up the issues to be mailed. The press broke down (it always did), and Randall had to change into a jump suit he kept handy, to help Salton Sims get it back into operation.

Few of the production troubles disturbed the reporters' room. Catherine was profoundly thankful. She felt she had had as much emotion, other peoples' and her own, as she could deal with for a while. She lay low deliberatly, not looking up from her desk at all, if she could help it.

The telephone didn't ring. People in Lowfield knew that Tuesday afternoon was frantic in the production department at the paper, and they generally supposed the reporters were busy too. In fact, the reporters regarded Tuesday afternoon as semilegitimate goof-off time.

When Catherine wasn't poking around figuring out column inches for the next issue, she was staring out the window by her desk, watching people come and go from the courthouse and the shops around the square. She was daydreaming, half-awake, lulled back into a sense of the continuity of the town by the normal sights of ladies coming and going from the grocery, storeowners and their customers chatting in front of the shops, and a town policeman working his way around the square with painstaking slowness, giving out parking tickets. The policeman was preceded by the usual flurry out of the stores and the courthouse as people saw him coming and hastily moved their cars to safety, or added more coins to the meters.

Catherine's thoughts inevitably drifted to Melba Barnes. She wondered what Sally would say if she knew her mother had accused Catherine, her high school buddy, of having an affair with Sally's father. Then she wondered what Jewel would say, and had an inward tremor of amusement as she imagined Jewel's pungent comments.

Catherine couldn't help feeling pity for crazy Melba Barnes. She tried to picture herself married and suspecting her husband of having a woman on the side. She couldn't quite think herself into it, but she felt a strong distaste at the idea.

It was the stealthy aspect of adultery, the sneaking and concealment in the face of someone close to you, that made it seem so . . . slimy. Though I suppose, Catherine reflected, the sneaking is more fun than the actual bedding down, for some people.

The extension on her desk buzzed. Catherine tucked the receiver between ear and shoulder; she was gathering loose paper clips to shove them into their original box.

"I'm sorry," whispered a voice, and the line went dead.

Melba Barnes was apologizing as abruptly as she had accused. Catherine returned the receiver to its cradle. She wondered whether Mrs. Barnes had ever called Leona and made the same accusations. Catherine wished she hadn't had that particular idea. Perhaps Melba hadn't stopped at words, with Leona.

No, quit it, Catherine admonished herself. When will I be able to stop assessing murderous potential in everyone I speak to? When will people stop wondering about my own potential for violence?

My life was so *simple*, she thought wearily. Now I'm operating upside down.

She was glad when Tom strode into the room, clutching a copy of the newly printed paper, half-wrathful and half-amused over a typo he hadn't caught in one of his stories.

A local girl had been elected Miss Soybean Products of Lowfield County—amusing enough in itself, at least to Tom. Miss Soybean Products was in law school, which had been misprinted "lay" school. Catherine laughed over this bad joke until Tom threatened to throw water in her face.

"Extended hilarity," Tom said sarcastically, when Catherine's giggles had finally trailed off, "is just not your style, Miss Linton."

That pomposity was enough to set Catherine off again. Leila, attracted by the unaccustomed laughter from Catherine's corner, appeared in the doorway and looked questioningly until Tom smiled at her.

Leila swept back to her desk, mollified, her bare legs looking revoltingly long and elegant to Catherine's envious eyes. Tom was transparently gloating as he watched Leila's retreat from a rear view. He hummed and whistled the rest of the afternoon, and wasn't as angry as Catherine had supposed he would be when he phoned the garage and found that his car wasn't ready. In a resigned voice, he asked her for a ride home.

"Of course," she said. "Is it time to go?"

"When are you going to start wearing a watch?"

"When I can remember to put it on in the morning," she answered instantly.

"You never wear jewelry," Tom observed with a note of disapproval. "You ought to; you ought to wear silver. It would look good with your hair."

Catherine mulled that over. If she was going to buy new clothes and new curtains and a new bedspread, to say nothing of her decision to cut down the hedge, why not some jewelry? She had always been so indifferent to it that her parents had stopped giving it to her.

I have nice ankles, she thought, peering at then. Maybe an anklet. Or were anklets hopelessly unfashionable?

And that was the most serious thought she had for the rest of the afternoon.

Sometimes on Tuesday afternoons she and Tom performed necessary housekeeping chores, like cleaning the darkroom or weeding out old files of pictures, but today neither was in the mood.

Tom kept up a pretense of occupation, in case Randall walked through, by pulling out the files containing the weekly columns. Every Tuesday, he made a little ceremony out of clipping the columns for the next issue. Catherine suspected he read the monthly allocation of comic strips in a single sitting. This little task could easily have been left to the production foreman, but Tom had somehow appropriated it when he came to the *Gazette*; and no one cared enough to take it out of his hands.

For the rest of the lazy afternoon, with the sun cutting through the venetian blinds across the big window, casting patterns on the floor, Tom read Catherine snips from the weekly columns ("Dr. Croft," "Harry's Home Tips," and "Sandra Says") and from the mailed-in stories the *Gazette* received from state departments and the government.

Catherine listened with half an ear, smiled occasionally, cleaned out her desk at a snail's pace, and watched the bars of light and shadow shift across the floor. Randall came through once, filthy with grease and ink from the press, his pipe clenched between his teeth. He reached out to pat Catherine's hair as he walked past (Tom's back was turned, to show the boss he was busy), and Catherine dodged his grimy hand and laughed silently as he made a mock-threatening swipe at her face.

She was glad when it was time to go. She told

Tom, as they drove home, that she planned an exciting evening of house-cleaning.

"Damn, I'd better clean my bathroom," he said, suddenly anxious.

"Got a date with Leila tonight?"

Tom grinned and said, "My lips are sealed. I have to protect the lady's good name. But I wonder how Randall feels about staff members dating each other."

He looked at Catherine blankly when she began to laugh.

"I swear, you've changed," he said huffily. "It used to be as much as I could do to wring a smile out of you."

Being turned upside down had brought the lightest as well as the heaviest elements in her to the top, Catherine decided, as she pulled into her driveway.

I guess when all this settles I might come out very different, she reflected.

"I never know *what* you're going to do anymore," Tom grumped.

"I don't either," she said. To their mutual surprise she patted him on the shoudler. "See?" she said shyly.

"Where will you stop in your mad excesses?" Tom asked dramatically. Then he grinned at her and gave her hand a squeeze.

"See you tomorrow," he said blithely.

She watched him stalk off across the lawn. He was pulling off his tie as he went. He cast a long narrow shadow across the grass.

In six hours he would be dead.

⁂

Catherine ate a brownie. There had been a coffee can at the back door when she unlocked it, a three-pound Folger's can full of brown bars. Even before she found the note inside, she knew they were from Betty Eakins, the Lintons' former maid.

The note, written on a ragged piece of paper, read, "Miss Catherine, I thought you might like these right now. You use to. Come see me when you get a minute. Betty."

Catherine's eyes prickled when she thought of ancient Betty walking all the way to her house on arthritic legs. Then she shook herself briskly. Probably that young deputy son of hers had brought Betty in his car.

The brownies were as wonderful as Catherine remembered; but not much of a meal. She reminded herself to go to the grocery store on her lunch hour the next day. She decided to drive to Memphis on Thursday evening after work, to begin her spending spree. If Randall was taking her out to dinner and to a movie Friday . . . She had to rouse herself from thinking about clothes, and Randall, to begin her belated housecleaning.

She started by cutting off the air conditioning and opening all the windows. The cessation of the humming of the central-air unit made the house suddenly very quiet. Outside in the dusk the locusts had begun their nightly drone. Catherine stood at a window listening, caught herself at it, and was angry; but she checked the three doors into the house to make sure they were locked.

Catherine began her cleaning in the master bedroom. She put on her oldest jeans for the operation; she never failed to get dirty while the house got clean. She scrubbed the bathroom methodically, and then set about dusting. The house was full of bookcases and her grandmother's bric-a-brac, so it was nine o'clock by the time she put away the dust rag and pulled the vacuum cleaner from its closet. The vacuum's businesslike roar filled the house with a satisfying sound, and Catherine maneuvered it around the rooms with unusual care, shifting the furniture laboriously to reach every corner and cranny.

Kitchen floor next, she decided as she looped the vaccum cord. And then I'll be through.

This evening was a little cooler than the one before, but her shirt was clinging to her back and her forehead felt wet by the time she had moved the chairs around the kitchen dining table.

The good thing about cleaning, she thought, as she turned on the kitchen-sink tap full blast, was that you could think about anything or nothing.

She chose to think of nothing, and the physical work was relaxing. But she was beginning to feel bored by the time she finished the tile floor.

She wrung out the dirty mop, rinsed, and wrung out the excess water again. Usually she put the mop out the side door to dry, but tonight she decided to put it out the back door. The last time, she had forgotten to bring it in for several days. In case she did that again, she wanted it to be out of sight from the street.

With a dirty kitchen towel wrapped around the mop to catch drips, Catherine walked quickly through the den and opened the back door to the night.

After propping the mop upright, she stood for a minute on the steps, looking up at the dark sky. It was cloudy; the stars were blotted out. Catherine hoped that meant rain, but the air didn't feel right for a shower. It was heavy, but not pressing.

As she stood with her face raised to the night sky, she heard a rustling in the grass.

She remained quite still. Her eyes, still turned sky-ward, no longer saw the blackness above them. They were blind with concentration. Everything in her was bent on identifying the source of the sound, so like that of feet passing through dry grass.

She thought of the light streaming from the open door behind her; of her outline, presented clearly to whatever was out there in the night.

In that interminable moment she was reminded of dreams she had had as a child, dreams in which danger threatened. In those dreams, she could never decide whether moving with elaborate unconcern or moving like lightning would save her. Some nights she tried one thing, some nights another. Which now? she wondered.

The sound was not repeated. Whatever was out there, beyond the pool of light from her house, was standing as still as she was.

Waiting to see what I will do.

What will I do?

If I move fast, if I show fear, it will be on me, she thought.

The watcher assumed the dimensions of the phan-toms of her dreams, enormously big and perpetually hungry—and too awful to have to face.

She turned very quietly and without haste, opened

the screen door and stepped inside her house. Very quietly and without haste she shut the heavy wooden door behind her. Then with fingers that were not at all quiet and were extremely hasty, she locked the door and leaned against it. She slid down the door until her rear hit the floor, and there she stayed until her breathing became more regular.

Should I call the police. To say what? I heard something in the grass and I'm scared, Sheriff Galton. I heard something in the grass . . .

And though she was sharply and clearly glad that no one would ever know she was doing it, she crept on her knees to the nearest window and huddled below it to listen.

A dry whisper in the grass. It had resumed movement.

She raised her head cautiously and peered through the screen. In the light from the window, she saw a bird hopping through the yard. As she watched, it triumphantly pulled a bug from the grass and hopped away with its prey.

"Goddamn! Don't you know you're supposed to be asleep?" she asked the bird hoarsely. It was understandably startled and flew off, taking care to retain the bug even in its fright.

Catherine expelled a long breath and slumped

against the wall. As she was about to give a self-conscious laugh at her panic, she changed her mind. It wasn't funny.

I don't care that I looked crazy as hell, she told her inward critic. I really don't care.

She sat there for a few minutes, letting her body calm down gradually.

"Oh boy," she said. "Oh boy."

She had just scrambled clumsily to her feet when she heard a faint, curious buzz.

She turned her head to one side, trying to identify the source of that half-familiar sound.

The buzz came again, after she had hesitantly started down the hall to her bedroom in obedience to an obscure urging that told her it was the right place to go.

The second time she heard the sound, she recognized it.

It was the buzzer in her father's old office.

Someone's calling for him, but he's not here, she thought. He's dead.

Her skin crawled.

For a third time the buzzer made its rasping appeal.

"It's *Tom*," she said out loud. Tom. Playing a stupid joke.

But he had promised he wouldn't. She couldn't

recall him breaking a promise. He had been so serious when she had told him never to play a joke on her
with the buzzer.

Something was wrong.

When she reached the master bedroom, she half
expected to see her father's head rising sleepily from
his pillow in answer to the summons from his office.

She stared at the place where the sound of the
buzzer issued, by the bed on the side where her father
had slept.

He's calling me, she thought. *Tom* is calling me.

The buzzer fell silent.

Tom, she told herself with an effort. Not Father.

"I am not a fool," she said. She pulled open the
drawer of her bedside table, grabbed her gun, and ran
back down the hall.

Catherine didn't think of the fear that had just let
go of her ankles. She was needed, and she had to go,
to run, to get there before it was too late.

Out the back door. Fumble with the light switch
that would illumine that terrifying yard. A quick scan
after the light was on.

The yard was empty.

Running through the grass, avoiding the stepping-
stones that would have tripped her in her haste.
Through the hedge that seemed to clutch at her.

She was almost at Tom's back door when she saw
that it was wide open. She stopped so suddenly that
she wobbled back and forth, and had to struggle to
keep her balance. A faint light glowed from the open
rectangle. The door ajar to the hot night confirmed
her feeling that something was horribly wrong. She
held her gun ready.

Not even the eerie sound of the buzzer had been
as frightening as that open door was. As she crept
closer, she could feel the rush of cooled air escaping
from the house.

She eased open the screen door as quietly as she
could. It creaked a little and she held her breath.

⁂

The doors all along the short hall were shut. The faint
glow was coming from the living room, and she was
looking at it so fixedly that she failed to see the red
splotches against the hall's white paint, until a thread
trickled down from a larger splash. Its tiny movement, slow and hesitant, caught the corner of her eye.
She stared at it and wondered if she could move.

There was no sound in the house except the hum of
air conditioning behind one of the closed doors. The
night, let in through the back door, held its breath.

Because she had to, she began to go forward, her

hand against the wall for support. She snatched it away when it encountered wetness.

The hall resembled every nightmare she had ever dreamed. But the thing in the grass had gotten some-one else instead of her.

As she moved closer to the light, closer to the living room, her scalp began to crawl.

"Tom?" she whispered.

The living room was a shambles. This disorder in what had been so neat struck her first. She didn't see Tom for a moment; then she saw his legs, his long thin legs, extending beyond the trunk that had served as his coffee table.

Without realizing she had moved, she was suddenly standing by him, looking down. He was on his back. He was very still, but blood was still running from his wounds. She watched a drop run down his cheek, over what had been his cheekbone. She watched it very carefully until it hit the thin carpeting and was ab-sorbed in a larger stain.

"Oh Tom," she said, and her fear was swallowed up by her grief. She dropped the gun on the trunk, knelt on the soaked carpet, and put her fingers to the pulse in his neck. It throbbed for a second that was a lifetime, and then the faint throb died.

There was a stillness about him, the total absense

of movement that belongs only to the dead, after even the tiny motions of breathing are extinct.

I'm too late, she thought. She could feel the blood soaking through the denim covering her knees. I'm too late.

He was only wearing his trousers, and Catherine wanted to cover him up. He would hate everyone to see him like that, she thought. He would just hate it. And no one should see his face; I should not have seen his face.

There was a tiny movement at the edge of her vision.

Her head snapped up, and she was staring into Leila's face. As she watched, that face stretched oddly.

"Oh Leila, he's dead," Catherine said in an involuntary whisper. "He just died."

She rose to go to the girl, and Leila's silent scream came out in a weak strangled ache of a sound. Catherine reached out to touch her, then looked at her hand. It was bloody.

"Get away from me!" Leila shouted, her voice becoming unchained. She backed against the wall with her arms stretched out to repel Catherine. Then she realized she had put her back against a smear of blood, and her scream ripped the room apart.

Catherine suddenly realized that Leila thought she

had killed Tom. She also absorbed the peculiar fact that Leila was in her underwear.

The sound Leila made affected Catherine like alcohol in a cut.

"Stop it!" she said harshly, but Leila kept on. Catherine's exasperation was heightened by shock. She felt positive joy in applying the classical method for dealing with hysterics. With no compunction at all, she hit Leila as hard as she could, and only felt a flash of dismay when she saw the girl stagger a few feet, from the force of the blow.

I didn't know I was that strong, she thought in amazement. I guess I've never hit anyone before in my life.

The blow did indeed silence Leila, but it didn't calm her in the least. Her terror was evident in her trembling body and distended eyes.

"I didn't do it," Catherine said flatly.

But Leila was not in her right mind. Her eyes were empty of reason.

Catherine was irrationally angry.

"You stupid bitch! I didn't do this! I found him like this!"

Leila seemed to return to her body. She pointed a shaking finger at Catherine's bloody hands.

"From the hall," Catherine explained. "The buzzer

sounded." She pointed to the buzzer on the door frame. There was red spattering the wall around it. "You remember the buzzer. To the house. That my father used. I think Tom hit it in the struggle."

Leila looked where Catherine's finger was pointing. Her family had gone to Dr. Linton. She nodded slowly, looking as if she finally understood. She deflated as fear of her own death left her, but she stared at Tom's legs, her complexion changing from ashy brown to green.

"Are you all right?" Catherine asked ridiculously.

"I'm going to vomit," Leila muttered.

Catherine was thankful for her knowledge of the house, for she swung the girl into the bathroom and over the toilet just in time. Shivering now with reaction, Catherine sat on the edge of the bathtub until Leila emptied her stomach.

"I've got to call the police," Catherine said.

"Not from here," Leila pleaded. She was a limp ghost of herself.

"No," said Catherine, her own stomach heaving at the thought of staying there.

⚜

Catherine's courage was fast seeping away. But the need to get the younger girl out of the house, the responsibility for someone in worse shape than she herself was, kept her mind moving.

"We have to go over to my house," she said. "Can you walk?" A stupid question, she reflected, because Leila will just dammit have to walk, whether she thinks she can or not.

"Come on," Catherine said, "if you're through throwing up."

Leila got to her feet with some assistance.

Catherine awoke to another need.

"Clothes," she said sharply.

Leila looked down at herself and turned from green to red.

I didn't know people could turn so many colors, Catherine thought.

"Oh, Catherine," Leila began miserably.

"I don't give a damn," Catherine interrupted, "but I think no one else needs to know. Are your clothes in the bedroom?"

Leila nodded.

The bed was rumpled and Tom's shirt and under-wear were set neatly on a chair. Leila's dress was on the floor, her shoes under it.

Dress, shoes. Underwear; Leila had that on. Hose? No, she didn't wear them. What else? Purse, of course. Purse. For an awful moment, Catherine thought that it must be in the living room, until she spotted it by the side of the chair. She scanned the little bedroom for any other traces of Leila, but saw none. It might not hold up, but it was all she could do. Then she remembered her own possession in the house. She had to go into the living room after all. She went directly to the gun, grabbed it, and ran out.

Leila was slumped on the edge of the bathtub.

"Here," Catherine said crisply. She helped Leila into the dress and sandals and kept charge of the purse.

"Come on."

She got Leila to her feet. Leila was by far the taller of the two. It was awkward for both of them, in a horribly comic way. Catherine put her arm around Leila's waist, and Leila put hers around Catherine's neck. Somehow they supported each other down the spattered hall, out the open back door, and across the yard. They had to go slowly, tottering like two drunks through the gap in the hedge.

"I'm afraid," Leila whispered, and the dark between the houses suddenly held ominous possibilities that Catherine had forgotten in her haste to leave the abattoir that had been Tom's home. She was hopelessly burdened. Leila and Leila's purse would make her too slow with the gun.

Catherine felt Leila begin to shake again, and

heard the girl's breath become more like sobbing. They would never make it if Leila collapsed. Catherine was coming to the end of her strength. I will go mad if Leila screams again, she thought.

"Come *on*," Catherine hissed through clenched teeth. Leila's arm around her neck was pinning her hair down, and the pain kept Catherine from panicking.

She had to use every muscle she possessed to haul Leila up the steps to her den. She dumped the girl on a couch and wobbled into the kitchen. She didn't sit down while she dialed the police, but leaned against the wall. She knew that if she sat down she would not be able to get up, and something still had to be done for the girl in her den.

By now Catherine almost hated Leila.

She said something, she never remembered what, into the telephone when it was answered at the sheriff's office. She hung up when an excited voice began to ask questions. Then she dropped her gun into a handy drawer. Before she returned to the girl, there was something she was going to do for herself.

She fumbled with the tiny Lowfield telephone directory, opening it with ponderous care to the "G" page. She read the numbers out loud to herself and dialed with that same nerve-wracking slowness.

He answered the telephone himself.

"Randall," she said, enunciating very deliberately. Then she was unable to speak.

"Catherine?"

"Randall . . . I wish you would come. Tom is dead."

The silence was full of questions he was not going to ask yet.

"Tom is dead," she repeated, and carefully hung up the phone, because she was afraid she was going to say it again.

She wondered what she had been planning to do next. Then she remembered Leila, and looked around the kitchen for something to take the girl. The most useful thing she could see was a roll of paper towels.

I think this is shock, she told herself. With precise movements, in slow motion, she picked up the roll of paper towels and began her slow trip back to the den.

As it turned out, the towels were a good idea. Leila had dissolved in tears by now, and she began choking out her story almost incoherently when Catherine reappeared.

Catherine handed Leila the roll, or rather simply thrust it into the girl's lap. She debated whether or not she could now sit down, and decided she could.

She sat by the weeping girl and fixed a wide gray gaze on the pretty face now fuzzy with tears.

"We had a date," Leila choked, "but his car was in the shop, so I had to drive over to his place, but I parked the car a block away because I didn't want anyone to tell Mama and Daddy, you know how people here tell your parents everything . . ."

Catherine automatically ripped a towel off the roll and stuffed it into Leila's hands. Leila looked at it as if she had never seen one, and used it.

"Oh, I loved him so much, and he was so good-looking . . . You know how it is . . . I just couldn't help it." A pause for another application of the towel. "And then when we were in bed, I mean, after it was over, there was a sound in the hall—"

I hope it was good for Tom, Catherine thought clearly. It better have been good.

"—and he got up and put on his pants, and he told me to stay quiet, not to move. He just whispered right up close to my ear, I was so . . . *scared* . . . 'I left the damn door unlocked,' he said."

Leila turned her ruined face to Catherine, and her long hand gripped Catherine's frail wrist with painful strength.

"He went out and then I heard sounds, oh God, sounds. They hit the walls and came off them, out in the hall and then in the living room. I heard things falling and turning over. I thought there must be five people out there, I swear to God. And I couldn't keep quiet any more, I screamed. And I thought someone ran out of the house. So I waited for Tom to come get me. I thought he'd come in and say it had been a *burglar*. When he didn't come back, I thought he was calling the police. And I wanted to get up and get dressed before they got there. But I couldn't . . . I was too scared. I waited and waited, and I couldn't hear anything. So then I put my underwear on, as quiet as I could. I thought at least I could start getting ready. And then I heard the screen door. And it was you. I thought it was the man coming back. I guess it was a man. But I couldn't *wait* anymore. I had to see. I couldn't wait for Tom anymore."

Sirens and lights outside.

The difference was that this time Randall was there, and his mother Angel. Randall only left Catherine once, to identify Tom formally. Angel made coffee and more coffee. And she greeted Leila's parents and led them to their weeping daughter.

Catherine observed dryly that Leila had recovered enough wits to protect herself: the girl edited her story to say that she and Tom had been sitting in the living room when they heard the noise of someone prowling, and that Tom has hustled her into the bedroom for her protection. That left open the question of why Tom hadn't called the police from the telephone in the living room, but Catherine decided that on the whole Leila had done well.

Then it was Catherine's turn.

She was holding an embroidered pillow in her lap. She remembered her mother's hands setting in the stitches. She had moved it from its place in the corner of the couch, so that she could jam herself into that corner as tightly as possible. The couch protected her right side and her back, and Randall was a solid wall on her left. Her fingers went over and over the embroidery her mother had worked on for hours. While Sheriff Galton asked her questions, her fingers never quit moving, in contrast to her face, which felt stiff, as if it didn't fit her skull very well.

Why had she not heard the screams Leila said she had given?

Because if Leila was shut in the bedroom, I wouldn't.

Why had she gone over to the house?

I heard the buzzer, he was calling me. I was too

late. I heard a rustle in the grass, before the buzzer went off.

Why hadn't she called the police?

I thought it was a bird. I guess now it was— whoever . . .

She was grateful for Randall and his mother, but she had gone where Randall could not reach her. She knew he was there, she felt his warmth and knew he was supporting her. She knew Angel was smoothing the way with cups of coffee and her mere presence, for Angel Gerrard, with her erect figure and carefully tended white hair, was a strong and influential woman and an impressive ally.

Catherine desperately wanted to reach out to them, to talk to them, to touch Randall's broad hand, but she could not. She looked at them from the corner of her eye. When they looked at her, she turned away: for suspicion hung around her like the heavy summer air.

She saw it in the eyes of the police, she saw it in the way Leila's parents carefully ignored her.

She heard one of the deputies ask Leila if the clothing Catherine was wearing now was the same she had worn when Leila saw her kneeling by Tom's body. She saw the deputy look at the blood dried on her knees, and at the smears on her hand.

No one would look directly at her face.

People might accept that she had happened to find one body, but not two, Catherine saw.

Not that she had been first on the scene two times.

Not that she had reported two murders. In three days.

The bruise forming on Leila's face, where Catherine had hit her, was examined by suspicious eyes. Leila had included the blow in her recital, and she had been quite graphic in describing how she was knocked to the wall by the force of Catherine's open hand.

Catherine saw very clearly that her frame was being reassessed with regard to its strength.

In a sideways glance, Catherine saw Angel Gerrard's back get stiffer and stiffer during Leila's account. A gleam entered Angel's alert brown eyes.

"I wonder how soon you can fire that girl?" Angel said very quietly to Randall, when the room was momentarily emptied of all but the three of them.

"I won't wait too long," Randall said grimly. There was a rough edge to his voice that Catherine had never heard before.

"Of course she was in bed with the boy," Angel said briskly. She looked at Catherine for confirmation.

For the first time, Catherine met Angel's eyes directly. She nodded.

"I thought so," Angel said. "She's a pretty thing, but she has the brains of a gourd. I wonder that she manages to file things correctly."

"She doesn't," Randall said.

"Catherine," Angel said sharply.

Catherine kept her face averted.

"Look at me, girl," Angel said more sharply.

Catherine did, and felt as if she had gotten a shot of amphetamine.

"Did you hit that girl?"

"Yes," Catherine replied.

"Good. Now wipe that guilt off your face. None of us thinks you had anything to do with this."

Randall's arm tightened around her shoulders, and he gave her a little shake, as if to jog her circulation back into action.

She began to feel warm. The sluggishness of strain and fear were slowly draining away.

Sheriff Galton came in the back door. He looked haggard, years older. He seemed so ill that Catherine was on the verge of urging him to see a doctor, when she realized how ludicrous that would sound.

The sheriff dropped into a chair and looked at her wearily.

"Did Tom tell you that he knew anything about Leona Gaites's murder?"

"You know how he was," she answered. "He made big noises about digging into it and finding out something that you-all didn't know. But I don't think it came to anything?"

"You sure? He said nothing to you about finding something?"

"Not to me."

"Well," Galton muttered, passing a huge hand over his face, "there's that marijuana in his house. Maybe something to do with that."

Why didn't I remember to take that with me? Catherine thought. Then she remembered that Tom had bought the dope from James Galton Junior. She exchanged a quick look with Randall and hunched deeper in the sofa. Angel caught the exchanged glance, and rose to go to the kitchen to replenish the coffeepot.

"You know anything about that marijuana?" Galton asked her.

Now she was in a corner.

"I don't think Tom's death has anything to do with that," she said.

"Am I going to have to search your house, too?"

"I saw it in his house when I went there Sunday,"

she said. "He told me he had bought it locally. That's all I know."

The sheriff might not be admitting to himself what his son was doing, but Catherine could see that he knew. When he heard the word *locally*, he ran his hand over his face again.

"Where's Tom's car?" he asked abruptly.

"In the shop; Don's," she said.

"It would look like Tom wasn't home," Randall observed.

Catherine turned and looked at him. Sheriff Galton nodded slowly.

"Especially with the lights off, just the one light on in the living room," Galton thought out loud. "Maybe this was just breaking and entering that turned into something else when Tom came out of the bedroom unexpectedly."

But his voice held no conviction.

"I overheard that the wounds are similar to Leona's," Randall said expressionlessly. "Is that true?"

"Yes," said the sheriff. "Very similar. But then, in any homicide by beating with a blunt instrument, they would be."

A little idea began to trickle through Catherine's tired mind. But when she tried to focus on the tenuous thought, it dissolved. I should have let it alone, she thought. If I had let it alone, it would have formed.

"Drink," said Angel firmly, putting a full cup on the coffee table in front of Catherine.

She looked up at the older woman, amazed that Angel could be immaculate at such an hour. Then her eyes filled with tears of gratitude that Angel had come to support her. Catherine shook her head angrily. I'm getting maudlin, she thought. She bent forward to pick up her coffee and to hide her face.

"Whoever did this would have been covered with blood," Galton said, out of nowhere.

He looked at Catherine. Her eyes met his over the rim of her cup.

"I would not describe Catherine as exactly covered with blood," Randall said with a dangerous gentleness. She felt his body tensing.

"No," said the sheriff quietly. "I see that."

"Randall, do you have the Mascalco boy's home phone number? His parents' number, I mean?" Angel asked in the silence that had fallen.

"Oh. Oh God." He thought. "Yes, it's sure to be in the file at the office. He was living with them when he applied for the job. I'll have to go down and get it."

"You can give it to me," rumbled Galton.

"I'll call them," Randall said tightly.

"Then I don't envy you," said the sheriff. "I ought to do that myself."

"He was my employee," Randall replied.

"Okay, if you're sure. Tell them to call my office. I guess there's nothing more we can do here tonight. We've asked people for blocks around all the questions we can think of. No one saw a suspicious car, or any car except Leila's. No one heard anything, saw anyone. Well, come to the station tomorrow morning and make your statement, Catherine."

"Oh yes, I know the routine," she said flatly.

Maybe by then I'll have another dead body to report, she told herself. Gosh, maybe someone will be dead on my lawn when I go out to the car tomorrow morning. That way, I could knock off two statements at once. People should hire me as a divining rod, to find bodies.

She realized she had to get some grip on herself, or she wouldn't be able to do anything the next day. Or for weeks. The black hole into which she had fallen when her parents died was waiting for her. An indescribable abyss of depression confronted her. She had only to take one more step and she would fall in.

The fear began to grip her. But fear would hurry her toward the hole faster than anything, if she let it overwhelm her. She wanted to lean against Randall with more than her body, but she knew from her experience during the weeks after her parents' death that this was something she had to fight through alone.

But Randall was there. When she came through, she would have a tenuous something at the other end. She hadn't had that before, and she had made it then. She would make it again. This time, if she won decisively, it might never happen again, she thought.

The police were gone. Angel was gone, after telling Randall without a twitch of an eyebrow that he would be staying with Catherine that night.

Only Randall and Catherine were left in the house, and it seemed empty with just two inhabitants, after the coming and going it had seen that evening.

In the house out back, there was fingerprinting dust, bloodstains, and silence. The blood, Tom's blood, would be dry now, and brown. Catherine could feel the presence of that house at her back. She wondered what she would do with it, the old house that had seen so many uses in its long life. Who would want it now?

Randall had gone to get the Mascalcos' telephone number after a long, quiet, tense discussion
with Catherine. He had not wanted to wake the Mascalcos with the news that their son was dead. He had
wanted to wait until morning. Catherine had only
thought they had a right to know as soon as possible.
It couldn't be withheld from them, she had argued.
They would bitterly resent being called in the morning and learning their son had been dead for twelve
hours.

Catherine had not learned of the death of her parents until she had gone back to her new apartment
from her new job. She remembered the guilt she had
felt at having been happily engaged in something
else while their corpses were in a little funeral home
in Arkansas. She remembered her anger that others
had known the news, more important to her than to
anyone in the world, hours before she was told.

Randall had yielded to her argument. She could
hear his voice in the kitchen now.

But she realized, as she huddled in her corner of
the couch, that she should have said nothing to Randall, nothing at all. He, not Catherine, was the one
who had volunteered to break the news. She should
have left it up to him, since he had taken on the sick-
ening responsibility.

She listened to the murmur of his voice and felt furious at her own interference. Her capacity for anger with herself was far greater than her capacity for anger with anyone else.

When Randall returned to the den, his face was gray with strain. He removed his glasses and rubbed the bridge of his nose. When he finally spoke, it was not about the conversation that had just taken place.

"Catherine, take off those goddamned clothes," he said.

She gaped at him.

Then she understood. She rose without a word. In the bathroom she yanked off the bloodstained jeans and jammed them into the garbage can. She looked down at herself and saw that the blood had soaked through her clothes and dried on her skin. She stepped into the shower and soaped and rinsed, then repeated, until her hands and legs were white again and chafed with scrubbing.

Tom's blood, down the drain. Four people, down the drain. Gone. Snuffed out like dogs hit by careless cars, because they were in the wrong place at the wrong time; because they weren't aware of the danger until it was too late.

Randall would hire a new reporter. He would doubtless start looking the next day.

Jerry Selforth was prescribing antibiotics and setting broken arms, just as Dr. Linton had done for years. He had a nurse who managed his office just as well as Leona would have. And Molly Perkins held the coffees for the bridge club every bit as well as Rachel Linton had.

Other dun-colored dogs were running through the fields, coupling with bitches to ensure more dun-colored dogs.

That was the way life went on. The thought might even be comforting, after a few years. Many years. More years than I will live, she thought.

She sprayed herself with perfume, thinking the smell of Tom's death was still on her, and went out to join Randall.

<hr />

He seemed to have recovered from the worst of his conversation with the Mascalcos. But for the first time, Catherine was fully conscious that he was twelve years older than she was. He had gotten out his pipe and was puffing away, looking more than ever like a muscular, misplaced professor.

"Can you sleep now?"

She shook her head.

"Neither can I. Let's go over it, if you can stand that."

She waited. She owed him this, for having urged him to call the Mascalcos.

"Leona. No—your parents. The first ones."

A fire ignited in her tired body. He accepted her conviction. He agreed.

"Your mother. Your father. His nurse. A reporter who said he was going to pry into their murders. This started with your folks. Glenn or Rachel, as the primary target?"

"I think . . . my father."

"I agree. Something he knew as a doctor."

"Not necessarily," she said. "He was a friend to half the county, and he inspired confidences."

"Granted." Randall knocked his pipe out in an ashtray. "Do you think Leona could have killed your parents? Could she have been a murderer? How did she feel about your father?"

"Before she was a blackmailer and an abortionist, she was a good nurse for my father for thirty-odd years," Catherine replied. "There was never anything between them, but I think Leona loved my father. I can see that now . . . Maybe I knew it all along."

"Do you think she could have killed him, knowing she couldn't ever have him?"

"I don't think so. I think she was used to the companionship she had with him every day at the office. She would have been his nurse until he retired, and that was years away. And she lost her income when he died: Leona loved money, too. Last point, but not least, I don't think she knew how to tamper with a car."

"That's disposed of, then." Randall had tidied that argument away. Catherine realized that in his own way he was working off the grief and horror of Tom's death.

"So," he muttered, "we assume that Leona didn't kill your parents. Do we take for granted, then, that Glenn, Rachel, and Leona were killed by the same person, for the same reason?"

Sure, why not? Catherine thought crazily. She nodded.

"Okay. That would point to something they all knew. Considering the six-month lapse between murders, it would seem that for six months Leona kept silent about something she knew, while the murderer paid her blackmail money. Something Leona discovered after your father was killed, maybe when she got the office wound up . . . Or maybe she realized the significance of an event or a conversation later. Something your father knew in his professional life; or something told to him in the office, as a friend."

Catherine mulled that over.

"I didn't express that well. Too many 'somethings' and 'maybes' . . . But do you agree?" Randall prodded.

Finally Catherine nodded. "Leona was always at the office when my father was there," she said slowly. "Even when someone buzzed him late at night"—she shuddered—"he would call her to come in before he even went over there. So she would have heard everything he heard, unless the conversation took place after he sent her from the room, while he talked with a patient after an examination. He would do that so she could prepare for the next patient, or pull files on whoever was in the waiting room. And all the files were accessible to her." Catherine stopped to think. "But with something like this, Randall, I can't imagine . . . We're presuming a critical conversation, a very personal and important conversation. Father would have sent Leona from the room. I know. He always knew when people were embarrassed or self-conscious about what they had, or suspected they had. His consultations with them were always private."

"Couldn't she have listened at the door?"

"It would have been hard. There were always other patients around, and the office maid, and the receptionist."

"Okay—difficult, but not impossible. However she did it, she found out. And Tom must have found out the same thing. You know what a gung-ho investigative reporter he thought he was. He wanted to solve this case before the police did. He told me so himself, Monday, while you were in Production."

Again the little thought moved at the back of Catherine's mind, and again she tried to catch hold of it too soon. It melted away.

"I don't know," she said uncertainly.

Randall looked at her questioningly.

"I would swear that during the past twenty-four hours he was thinking more about the breakup with his fiancée, and getting Leila to bed, than he was about Leona's murder," Catherine said. She gripped the embroidered pillow and added, "He was just a boy. He was younger than I am."

Randall touched her cheek. They sat in silence for a few minutes.

Then he said, "Just one more thing. If Leona knew who killed your father, do you think she would have kept quiet about it?"

"If she believed the person she was blackmailing was his murderer—she may not have known that, come to think of it—she might have figured, 'Dead is dead. What good can this bring me?' Even if she loved him. Or she might have thought she was getting some kind of vengeance by blackmailing the murderer."

Then Catherine added, "I realize now that I never knew Leona, never understood her. At all."

Randall stirred and looked at her. "You should be in bed," he said. "Are you going to be able to sleep?"

She nodded.

"I'll sleep in here," he said, thumping the couch.

"No."

"Catherine," he said gently, "this isn't the right time."

"I know that," she said irritably. "But you can sleep in my bed without being overcome by passion, surely, tired as we both are? Or you can have the other bed, in my old room."

"Even as tired as we are," he said, "I think I'd better take the other bed."

12

WHEN SHE GOT up the next morning he was
gone.

He had pulled the bed together, she found, when
she peeped shyly into her old room. She was disappointed but a little relieved. She would have liked to
see his head on the pillow, but her soul craved the
solitude of her coffemaking and reading at the table.

That might be a problem later, she thought hopefully.

He had left a note in the kitchen, propped against
a full coffeepot. Bless him, she thought, peering at
his spiky scrawl.

"Don't come in to work," Catherine read. "I
looked in at you this morning and had to overcome a

mighty temptation, but you need sleep more than anything else at this point." She smiled.

She saw through the steam of her first cup of coffee that it was nine o'clock. She had to go to the sheriff's office to make her statement, but she was going to take her time. She needed to collect herself before facing Sheriff Galton.

Of course she would go in to work after that. She knew Randall would be run ragged if she didn't show up. No reporters, no one to answer the phone, since Leila undoubtedly would not come in. And that telephone would be ringing off the wall.

Yes, she would go to work.

After she had had some coffee and a few cigarettes, she realized there was no use trying to make anything normal of the morning. How deeply I'm embedded in my little rut, she thought. A friend of mine died last night, while I was watching, and I try to drink my X number of cups of coffee, smoke X number of cigarettes, and stick to my piddling little routine.

She got dressed and drove over to the little brick building in front of the jail.

It was like her arrival there Saturday morning. To her horror, she began shaking as she pulled onto the concrete apron in front of the swinging door. She knew what she would see, and she saw it. There was Mary Jane Cory, typing, her unrealistic hair sprayed into an elaborate structure of swirls.

But the pattern was broken, after all, when the black deputy, Eakins, came out of the sheriff's office and approached her.

"Miss Linton," he said reluctantly, his voice hardly more than a mumble. Catherine turned to face him and waited cautiously.

"My mother wants to see you." Before Catherine could say anything, before she could tell him she didn't have any time that day, he went on. "She wants to see you awful bad. She's been on at me about it for two days now."

"What is it about?" She guiltily remembered the note in the can of brownies.

"She won't tell me. You know how stubborn and . . . old-fashioned she is."

"Old-fashioned" must mean "Uncle Tom," Catherine decided. Yes, Betty was. It made Catherine as uncomfortable as it made her son.

I just can't cope with Betty's "Miss Catherine's" this morning, she thought desperately. She was about to say no, when Percy Eakins gave her a pleading look it obviously hurt him to give. His pride was aching like arthritis on a rainy day, Catherine realized.

"I'll go after I make my statement," she said.

Then Mary Jane looked up from her typing, and Catherine became caught up in the mills of the law.

Catherine's statement was longer and a little tricky this time (since she was concealing something, though it seemed a harmless thing to conceal), and she had time to notice that Mary Jane was no longer sympathetic. She was, if possible, even more briskly professional than usual. Her eyes on Catherine's face were cold and speculative.

Catherine realized for the first time that this might be the pattern for the rest of her life, unless the murderer was caught. There was not enough evidence to arrest her: there was only the coincidence of two dead people turning up in Catherine Linton's immediate vicinity. The sheriff knew she couldn't have physically accomplished the murders, she thought. But that would make little difference in Lowfield talk.

She was so depressed when she left the sheriff's office that she figured going to see Betty Eakins couldn't make her feel worse.

The black part of Lowfield was as close to a ghetto as a tiny town could get. Some of the streets were unpaved, and the children ran and played in them, only reluctantly moving aside for cars to pass. Some of the houses were clean, neatly kept, and sound; but most of them leaned and staggered, barely able to contain the life that spilled out of them.

Betty's house was at a stage in between. It was still upright, but it was beginning to slide. The paint was peeling, and the yard was growing wild.

There were no sidewalks, of course, and the street, paved perhaps twenty years ago, was narrow. Catherine pulled as close to the house as she dared, and hoped no other car would want to pass while she was inside.

Children gathered on the other side of the street to watch her get out of the car. They ranged in age from three to ten, Catherine estimated, and their clothing was in various stages of disrepair, ranging from neat-but-dusty to out-and-out rags. They were barefoot, smiling, and shy. She gave them a tentative smile. The shyest covered their mouths with their hands, but let their returning grins shine through.

She pushed through the burgeoning sunflowers in the yard and knocked on the doorsill. The wooden door was open. The screen door was almost off its hinges.

"Who that?" came a creaky query from the darkness of the house's back rooms. The shades had been drawn against the heat.

"Catherine," she called.

"Miss Catherine!"

Betty's halting steps approached. Catherine could see her emerging from the kitchen. Betty must have been close to seventy-five. She was thin, bent, and gnarled. She was putting in her teeth as she walked, and was dressed in a formidably clean green and white housedress and white apron.

Catherine had never seen Betty without an apron on.

"Come on in! Come on in!" A chicken ran across the yard, and Betty made an automatic flapping gesture in its direction.

Catherine stepped into the room and looked around her for a place to sit. There was a sack of snap beans and a bowl half-full of prepared ones by a chair, so Catherine chose the sofa, which was covered by an old chenille bedspread, and lowered herself gingerly.

"You seen my boy this morning? He done told you I wanted to talk with you?"

"Yes, he did," Catherine said. "Thanks for the brownies. They were great. How are you feeling?"

"Getting old, getting old. My bones is hurting. But I reckon I'll live a while longer, make a few more batches of brownies."

Betty took up the sack of beans, then put it down when she remembered she had company.

"No, go on," Catherine said hastily.

Slowly Betty's hands returned to their work. Her head bent over the bowl. All Catherine could see was white hair braided and pinned in circles.

"Reckon I got to tell you something," Betty murmured. "You in trouble now . . . Reckon I got to speak up. I ain't told nobody, didn't want any trouble. But you my little girl. You in some kind of mess. I hear people talking."

The two women sat quietly. Catherine couldn't think of anything to say, and Betty was thinking about what to say next.

"That boy that got killed last night, was he your beau?"

"No," she said.

Betty looked up at her, relieved. "You got a beau?"

"Yes. Randall Gerrard," Catherine said firmly.

"Gerrard. I know Sadie who works for them. His daddy run the paper?"

"He's dead now. Randall runs it."

"The Gerrards got money? Is he good to you?"

"Yes."

"You know his mamma? She like you?"

"I think so."

"I went to your mamma and daddy's wedding. Your daddy," Betty said slowly. "He asked me to come. He said, 'You got to be there, Betty. It wouldn't be right without you.'"

Betty was building up to something, rambling around the corners of what she really wanted to say. Suddenly Catherine was curious.

"They've been dead about six months now," Betty said thoughtfully. "Nobody asked me any questions then. I was glad. Percy, he was trying to get on working for the sheriff. Little Betty ran off to Detroit about then. Left me her kids to look after. I had the woes of Job, seemed like. So when your folks died, I just didn't think about something I should've spoken up about. But then, no sheriff come asking *me* questions. That would've brought it to my mind. I would've spoken up. But—I just had too many other things worrying me."

Betty's fingers were moving steadily, breaking off the ends of the beans, then snapping them into pieces. Catherine watched the bowl fill up.

"But you in trouble now," Betty muttered. Her fingers stilled as she reached a decision. She looked up into Catherine's white face.

"You got a little sun on you for once, didn't you?" Betty observed. She cleared her throat. "Well, it was

this way. I never did like Miss Leona. I know"—
Betty lifted a dark hand to forestall an admonition
Catherine would never dream of giving—"it ain't up
to me to like or not like. God made us all, we all got a
place. But I didn't like her. I saw she didn't care for
you or your mamma. So I watched her close, when
she was in you-all's house. And even after I quit working for your mother, you know, I went and cleaned
your daddy's office when the woman who worked for
him got sick—or drunk, most often," Betty said se-
verely. She frowned over the erring maid for a moment.

"Here I am wandering," she resumed. "Well. About
three days before your folks got taken, I was over to
your daddy's office late in the afternoon. That Callie,
she had been on a long one, but you don't care about
that: it ain't the point of all this."

Catherine reached up to wipe the sweat from her
forehead, and found that her hand was shaking.

"Your daddy and some man was in the examination
room." Betty's eyes met Catherine's.

Catherine nodded jerkily.

"They was talking. They was raising their voices.
I knew something was wrong. I *never* heard raised
voices in your daddy's office before. It was late.
Wasn't no one there but me and Miss Leona." Betty's

face went wry with dislike. She heaved a heavy breath and went on.

"I was mopping the second examination room. My door was open, but the door to the other room, where your daddy and the man was, 'course it was closed. I could hear voices, but not what they were saying.

"I seen Miss Leona come along the hall, you know how quiet she moved in them white shoes. She passed by the door of my room. I wasn't making no noise; I don't think she knew I was there. She was 'spose to be gone. I heard your daddy tell her to go on home, he had seen everybody. But then I heard her messing 'round in the medicine room, and I guess she heard the other man come in and was so nosy she had to find out who it was. She didn't like nothing going on at that office that she didn't know all about. For that matter, she didn't like your daddy doing nothing if she didn't know what it was and why." And Betty shot Catherine a significant look with her yellowed eyes.

"What happened?" Catherine asked carefully.

"She was listening," said Betty. "She was listening at the door." Betty's voice was flat. "I knew that was wrong, your daddy wouldn't want that. Why else did he tell her to go home? But I couldn't *say* nothing."

Catherine could understand that. Betty would never have said anything to Leona.

"I put down my mop real quiet, and I went to the door of the room so I could watch her. She was just drinking it in. Her head was so close to that door you couldn't have got a broomstraw between them.

"Your daddy put his hand on the doorknob and opened it a little to leave, or maybe to tell the other man it was time for him to leave. Miss Leona stepped back right smart then, she sure did. She went and hid in your daddy's office. She didn't go by me, you see. She didn't see me," Betty emphasized. "I stayed where I was. I was scared, by that time. Your daddy, he wasn't mad, he was just upset . . . But that other man, he was *mad*.

"Your daddy took a step out of the room, but he stood with his back to me and talked some more. He says—I could hear him then—he says, 'You're going to have to face it. It's the law. I'm sorry, more sorry than I can say. But I have to report it. I got to tell . . .' This I didn't understand, Miss Catherine. Something about the government. Then he says, 'You know things have changed, it's not like it used to be. After a while, you can come home. No one need know. And you'll feel a lot better.'

"I didn't understand that part, either, Miss Catherine. The doctor said something about animals, some kind of animal. I don't remember the name of it. It was something they got in Texas, I know. I seen it on TV the other day, and when they call it by name, it was the same name. Begin with an *A*."

Aardvark? Catherine wondered incredulously. She rummaged in her mind for another animal whose name began with an *A*. Nothing. She pushed that aside, for Betty was still talking.

"—I stepped back where I was. I didn't want your daddy thinking I was listening in like Miss Leona. He went out the back of the office, all upset. He wouldn't have seen me if I'd jumped out in front of him and yelled. The other man, he came out after a minute. I heard him going down the hall and out the front door. So I didn't see him. I don't know to this day who it was. But Miss Leona knew, she saw him."

"And you didn't tell anyone," Catherine said.

"No. My Percy, my youngest, was worried about getting that job . . . Little Betty run off, leaving them poor kids. Your folks got killed. I forgot all about it until Miss Leona got herself killed. Then I heard you're in trouble, some folks think you did it. When you didn't come after I left you that note, I had Percy tell you I had to see you. All this may be nothing, Miss Catherine. But no one ever asked me. Now I think all the time. Remember, I can't go nowhere because of the arthritis."

Betty plodded through her multitude of excuses again. Catherine believed her. It probably hadn't seemed very important to her, except from the standpoint of warning her to watch out for Leona. And no one had asked Betty any questions.

"How close did you say this was to my parents' death?" Catherine asked.

"Three days, I think. I can't call to mind the day of the week. But three days, maybe two."

"And you're sure you don't know who the man was?" Catherine asked, knowing the answer.

"That's all I know, Miss Catherine."

"I have to go now," Catherine said shakily.

"Yes, ma'am."

"Don't say that," she said sharply. Then she collected herself. "I'm sorry, Betty. I'm glad you told me. I'll come again when I can."

"You bring that beau of yours by," said Betty, more cheerful now that her mind was at ease.

"I will, Betty. Goodbye. Thank you."

Catherine walked through the sunflowers in a daze.

The children were scattered in the street, playing an amputated form of baseball. Catherine automatically smiled at them, and drove out of the black section very slowly, to avoid chickens and children.

She didn't want to look in anyone's face right then.

She drove out of Lowfield a little way, just to the west of the highway where the last houses straggled to a stop. There was a small area full of trees, surrounded by a high metal fence. She turned into it, under the arch over the open gate, and parked her car in the usual spot. Beyond the fence, she could see a tractor in the fields. Except for that distant human, she was alone.

Lately she had not gone there as much as she had at first.

The headstones still looked new. The graves were neat. Catherine made donations to the church fund that paid the caretaker.

She had always liked it there, even as a child. She had read all the older headstones, and knew the more striking epitaphs by heart. It was always peaceful, always quiet.

She sat beside her family. Her parents were beside her grandparents. And her great-grandparents.

She sat beside them and cried.

When the big gush died down to occasional tears, and she was still shaky, but quieted, she walked through the cemetery. It was a good place to think without interruption.

She tried to picture Betty on the witness stand.

She couldn't.

She thought, *Antelope? Angus?*

Then she wiped off her face and returned to her car.

13

CATHERINE WAS IMMEDIATELY aware of the eyes. They peered from the door of the production room, and from the reception area. Two people were waiting there when she came in. They were obviously at a loss for what to do, without Leila at the desk to direct them. The door to Randall's office was shut, and the sound of typing came from behind it.

She felt a glaze harden on her face. She moved stiffly. One of the two visitors was an advertiser, delivering his ad for the next issue. He was startled by the sight of Catherine. Perhaps he had hoped to go back to the production room and have a good chat with the staff. Catherine took the ad and calmly assured him that she would deliver it herself.

The second visitor was the librarian, Mrs. Weilen-mann.

"I couldn't reach you at home," she told Catherine. "I just wanted you to know how much I'm—thinking of you."

"Thank you," Catherine said stiffly. "I can't talk about it, please."

Mrs. Weilenmann patted her on the shoulder, then left.

Randall's door opened.

"I thought it was you," he said. "Come in here."

She gestured toward the empty desk. "I ought to be out here."

"Mother's been handling it. She had to go out for a minute, but she'll be back."

When he had closed the door, he held her to him. Catherine looked past his ear blindly.

He released her and looked into her face. She slowly reached up to touch his cheek.

"You should have stayed at home," he said gently.

"No, no point in that."

"Things here are pretty unpleasant," he said.

He looked so depressed and so much older that Catherine was jolted into remembering something she had, incredibly, forgotten: that Randall feared Leona Gaites had been blackmailing his mother.

"Randall," she said tentatively, "surely you're not worried about Miss Angel?"

He looked at her uncomprehendingly.

"What? Oh, no. I did what you suggested. I just asked her. You were right. She said, 'No, if Leona Gaites had approached me with any such proposition, I would have told her to publish and be damned, and that she was welcome to use my paper to publish in!' I can't understand now why I even worried about it. I guess just knowing we had a skeleton in our closet, knowing Leona had been taking advantage of skeletons to make money . . ."

"Is there something else you're worried about?"

"Aside from hiring Tom's replacement, and wondering when I can expect that bitch Leila to come back, so I can get her to train a new receptionist?" he asked sharply. Then he shook his head. "I'm sorry, Catherine. I'm just tired. I want all this to be over. I want this town to return to normal. I want to have time to see you in a regular relationship, without the stress and blood all around us."

She wondered whether they would have become as close, if it hadn't been for those very conditions of stress and blood. She thought not.

"We can't worry about that now," Catherine said. "We have to wait for this to end. Then there'll be time to lie in the sun and go back to the levee. There's something I want to tell you, something I just found out."

Randall's extension buzzed at that second, and he bent over his desk to pick it up. He gave Catherine an exasperated look of apology.

While he spoke into the receiver, Catherine's gaze wandered over the collection of framed pictures and certificates covering the walls of his office. Four generations of Gerrard editors had occupied the room, so a great many of these mementos were yellowed. One piece of paper still white with freshness caught her eye.

"In appreciation of the services of Randall Gerrard and Dr. Jerry Selforth," Catherine read with difficulty, "from the Junior Baseball Club of Lowfield County."

I didn't know Randall and Jerry were coaches, Catherine thought idly.

She pictured Randall in uniform at the plate, hitting a ball over the bleachers, throwing down the bat and heading for first base.

Throwing down the bat . . . She stiffened. Before she could stop herself, another image arose: Randall's powerful arms swinging the bat at a blackmailing nurse, and at Tom. Maybe Leona hadn't approached

Angel Gerrard. Maybe she had approached Randall instead.

You fool, she lashed at herself savagely. Don't you dare think for one minute . . . After all baseball bats are hardly rare or hard to buy.

But how accessible the weapon was to Randall. How easily he could obtain that heavy length of wood, if he needed a weapon.

She knew her judgment was clouded by physical exhaustion and grief. She stared at Randall while he wrangled with the advertiser on the other end of the line.

If I'm wrong (and of course I'm wrong), he will never know I thought for one minute that he was connected with murder, she told herself.

Catherine lowered her eyes so they wouldn't meet Randall's inadvertently.

Maybe, just for now, I shouldn't tell him what Betty said, she reflected hesitantly. After all, her story is only confirmation of a half-baked theory of his, about Leona overhearing something at Daddy's office. It may not mean anything, right? And everyone who might have known something about this case is dead. Everybody but me . . . and Betty. Betty is the only possible living eyewitness to any portion of this whole chain of deaths.

Catherine realized she had just talked herself out of telling Randall about Betty's little story. She had reached a test of faith she couldn't pass.

Randall was still involved with his caller. Catherine tried to assume a natural expression and rose from her chair. When Randall glanced up inquiringly, she made typing gestures with her fingers. He nodded that he understood, and she eased out of his office. She moved toward her desk like an automaton and, once settled in her chair, folded her hands stiffly in her lap and stared at the wall. She was as miserable as she ever had been in her life.

When Randall's mother passed through the room, Catherine had to force herself to speak.

"Miss Angel," she said in a lifeless voice, "if you'd get me Tom's personnel file I'd appreciate it. I have to write a story."

Angel eyed Catherine sharply and then nodded briskly. She brought Tom's file to Catherine's desk, along with Randall's notes from his conversation with Jerry Selforth and the sheriff. Randall had been prepared to write the story if she had not come in, Catherine realized dully.

She rolled paper into the platen, flexed her tense fingers, took a deep breath, and began to type.

"Tom Mascalco, 21, a reporter for the *Lowfield*

Gazette, died Tuesday night as the result of wounds sustained in a struggle in his home."

When the story was almost finished, she had to buzz Randall to ask when Tom's funeral services would be held.

"Friday," he said wearily. "Holy Mary of the Assumption, in Memphis. Ten o'clock. We'll have to go."

It was the only time she spoke to him for the rest of the day.

⁂

During the afternoon, Sheriff Galton sent Deputy Ralph Carson to go through Tom's desk, to see if it contained any notes that might be regarded as clues. Ralph was courteous but remote. They might have barely known each other, instead of having dated off and on through high school, sharing hayrides, dances, and drinks. He was married now, with two children, Catherine remembered. But the gulf between them was far wider than the gap in time and circumstances.

He's definitely keeping his distance until he sees which way the cat jumps, she thought. But he has to be polite. After all, what if I didn't do it?

And provoking that courtesy, making him speak when he wanted to finish his job and leave, gave her an awful enjoyment.

The notes Tom had made on Leona's murder contained nothing that was not commonly known.

While Catherine identified items and notes to help the deputy, she also transferred *Gazette* material—sheets of columns and comic strips—to her own desk. She would have to handle that now.

As she gathered up the columns, she saw Tom leaning back in his chair, reading them with lazy interest, trying to decide which ones should be in next week's paper . . . pulling on his mustache, smiling, as he no doubt thought about persuading Leila to bed that evening.

For a moment her grasp weakened, and the sheets almost cascaded to the floor; but the next second she had hold of them again, and put them on her desk.

Then there was Tom's camera, in a bottom desk drawer. He had preferred to use his own, instead of the *Gazette*'s. It had film in it, she saw, and she realized she had to remove and develop the film before the camera could be returned to Tom's parents.

She thought of a question to ask Ralph Carson.

"About the house," she said abruptly.

He looked surprised.

"The one Tom rented from me," she explained. "What can I do about getting it cleaned? His parents will have to get in there to get his things out. They can't see that."

"Oh," he said. "Well, you could see if you could hire some prisoners from the jail to do it. Some trustees, maybe. They might be glad to do it for the money. Why don't you ask the sheriff?"

"I'll do that," she said, and they continued their fruitless sifting. All they found were a couple of magazines that made Carson turn red and caused Catherine to lift her eyebrows. She pitched them into Tom's wastebasket.

It was just as well, she decided, that she had gone through the desk instead of someone else.

When Carson left, his hands empty and his face glum, Catherine sat down at her desk and looked around aimlessly. She had to do something.

Her eyes lit on Tom's camera. She would develop the film in it. No one would bother her in the darkroom.

The reporters' tiny darkroom was to the left of the door that led to the production department. Catherine grabbed up the camera, buzzed Angel to tell her she was still incommunicado, and dived into the little room, turning on the red light that shone outside when film was being processed. Now no one could talk to her for a good length of time.

The smock she wore to protect her clothes from chemicals was hanging in its usual place on a hook on the door. Tom's heavy denim work apron was beside it. On an impulse, she ran her hands through the pockets of the apron. There was nothing in them, and her mouth twisted in self-derision as she let it fall back against the door.

She pulled on her smock, snapping it down the front, and looked around the darkroom to make sure where everything was before she turned off the lights.

While the film developed there was nothing to do but wait. Catherine lit a cigarette and propped herself against the high counter.

This was the nicest moment of a jarring day. She lounged in the eerie red glow, safe from intrusion because of the light shining outside the door. The *Gazette*'s little darkroom satisfied her catlike fondness for small places.

The "bing!" of the timer roused her from her reverie. She finished developing the film, her mind at ease and refreshed by the isolation and darkness.

Other places had big beautiful dryers, Catherine thought enviously. The *Gazette* had a clothesline and some clamps and a fan.

While the film was hanging from the clothesline,

drying, Catherine switched on the light and examined the half-used roll of film. The pictures were, as she had supposed, Tom's shots of the Lion's Club meeting, featuring its guest speaker, the lieutenant governor. In reversed black and white, Catherine saw shots of a speaker at a podium, and men seated in rows at a U-shaped collection of tables, the plates in front of them showing up as black circles.

Somehow, Tom's last pictures should have been of something more memorable, Catherine thought.

He had been by far a better photographer than she, but he had been too impatient to enjoy darkroom work. She had often developed his film while she did her own.

He made me feel like a regular Martha, Catherine thought: and despite her weariness and confusion, the peace of the little room relaxed her so that she could smile at the recollection. She was beginning to assimilate the fact that Tom was gone.

She decided to enlarge all the shots. It would take up time, while keeping her busy with something she enjoyed. And besides, she was not a good interpreter of negatives. Tom had been able to run a look down the film and choose this one or that one, as the best shots. Catherine had to put much more time and thought into picking out pictures.

She let out a sigh and set about enlarging the five shots Tom had taken. The *Gazette*'s enlarger was old and cranky, had been secondhand when purchased. But she had always felt she had a kind of silent understanding with the enlarger. And sure enough, today it cooperated.

As Catherine rocked the pictures in the developing tray, she decided that there was something romantic about photography. She watched, enthralled, as the faces began to emerge from the solution.

There was a dramatic shot of the speaker, bent over the podium, one arm extended in a point-making gesture. And operating on the theory that faces sold papers, Tom had taken several shots of the assembled Lions listening, with greater or lesser degrees of attention, to the address.

There was Sheriff Galton, looking bored. These past few days had made an awful difference in the man. Catherine focused on the face beside his: Martin Barnes, obviously daydreaming, perhaps about Jewel and her little house by the highway, she thought wryly. The mayor's face materialized. He was staring at a roll on his otherwise empty plate, perhaps wondering if anyone would notice if he ate it (he had been battling his paunch for years.)

There was Carl Perkins, smiling broadly, either at

the lieutenant governor's speech or at some private thought. Randall was beside him, pipe in hand. Then Jerry Selforth's smooth dark head appeared, his face all eagerness and attention. Jerry would marry a Lowfield girl, she decided, and stay there until he died.

⁂

When the pictures were ready, Catherine no longer had an excuse to linger in the darkroom. She emerged reluctantly, found Tom's copy of the story, and attached the picture of the lieutenant governor. She wrote the cut line and attached that. Then she typed in Tom's byline.

Once again she cast around for something to do.

There were the weekly columns she had lifted from Tom's desk. Clipping those columns was definitely necessary, and easy to do.

She got out her scissors and in a very few moments had cut out the comic strips indicated by date for the following week. The handyman column was easy, too. She imagined that the one about building rose trellises was suitable for summer, and her scissors snipped it out.

To prolong the little task, Catherine read all the Dr. Croft columns. There were seven left in this batch. The one in the previous week's paper had been on appendicitis. Catherine remembered that it had made Tom a little nervous, since he still possessed his appendix.

Well, here was one on Crohn's disease. What about that? Catherine scanned it and decided it didn't appeal to her.

Some of these are really exotic, she thought. Dr. Croft must be running out of ailments. My father would be glad of that.

Then her eye caught the word *Armadillo*.

***

She read the column through once, twice. Pity and loathing made her heart sick.

When she was able to rise, she went to the darkroom and upclipped Tom's Lion's Club group picture. She unearthed photo files from ten years ago, five years, two years. She leafed through them and laid a number of pictures side by side.

She understood now why her parents had died, why Leona and Tom had been beaten to death.

Her father had been an innocent. Leona had been foolish, criminally and fatally foolish. Tom had just been in the way.

The day of her parents' funeral passed drearily

through her mind again . . . And the day she and Leona had moved the filing cabinets into the attic of the old office. Leona hadn't taken a file from the cabinets that day, as Catherine had vaguely suspected after hearing Betty's story. Instead she had put something in; had hidden it there for safekeeping.

She had to produce it at least once, Catherine thought dully. To prove she had it; so she could get her damned money. She hid it because she was scared he would break into her house to steal it . . . She wouldn't have had any leverage after that. Didn't Leona know how desperate he was? Or was she blinded by greed? Maybe she did see blackmail as a way to avenge my father's death. She paid . . . He did break into her house to steal it, and he killed her in the process. He came prepared to kill her, with a baseball bat. What a convenient and appropriate weapon.

Catherine twisted her hair in a knot and held it on top of her head. She closed her eyes and thought of all the questions she had answered in the past few days without even being aware they had been asked. Her ignorance had caused Tom's death. That would be lodged in her conscience for the rest of her life.

Give the devil his due, she thought savagely. He didn't kill Leila. But then she was screaming, and he thought someone would come . . . Not enough time to kill Leila or search those cabinets . . . What a shock he must have had when she began yelling. It was bad enough that Tom was there, when he thought Tom was out on a date with Leila.

And of course he hasn't killed me, Catherine thought. He has tried every route in order to avoid killing me. He doesn't want to . . . He's *fond* of me. And he's probably very very *sorry* about Mother and Father. And Tom, my friend—too bad about Tom Mascalco. He was in the way. Of course, Leona asked for it.

Catherine shuddered.

Yes, very very *sorry* about Glenn and Rachel Linton.

It was a matter of pride and vengeance that she finish the thing herself. And a matter of habit: she had done things for herself for so long.

And then there was the fact that she had caused Tom's death. In the first place, she had given the murderer information indicating that Tom was an obstacle in his path; in the second place, she had not called the police when she had heard the rustling in the grass.

Her rational mind told her she had had nothing to do with the car troubles that had caused Tom to remain in the old office instead of going out with Leila; or with the couple's going to bed instead of using Leila's car to go to a movie, for example. But her rational mind also told her that words from her own mouth had led, however indirectly, to Tom's death.

Perhaps she could have saved Tom; nothing could have saved her parents.

When she thought again of the reason they had died, rage came over her. It had been gaining strength, quenching the pity and revulsion, while she sat brooding. The rage shook her as nothing had ever shaken her before. She felt as if she was being burned from the inside out.

She looked at the clock. She had forgotten about the time. Now she saw it was 5:30. Most of the staff must have gone by while she sat deaf and dumb.

Time to go, Catherine, she told herself.

She covered her typewriter and picked up her purse. She put the Dr. Croft column on Randall's desk, in silent apology. She thought of trying to find him. She was sure he was somewhere in the building, maybe in the production room working on the press with Salton. But a rising sense of urgency carried her out to her car.

She drove the short distance home with special care. She didn't trust herself.

She was so fixed on her course that she was bewildered when she saw a strange car with two people in it parked in front of her house. She saw two heads turning to follow her car into the garage, and realized she couldn't avoid finding out who they were and what they wanted.

As she walked across the lawn to meet them, she noticed the Tennessee license plate on their car. A man and a woman, middle-aged, attractive.

It was hard for her to understand what they were saying. Her ears weren't at fault, she discovered slowly; their voices were choked and hoarse. The pretty dark woman, still young, with the red-edged eyes, was Tom's mother, Catherine gradually realized; and the man with olive skin and light hair was his father.

Catherine's ingrained training triumphed in her handling of these newly bereaved parents. She acted out of sheer reflex, rising out of profound shock. She simply could not think of how to ask them to go away.

"Won't you come inside?" she asked.

"We don't want to trouble you, but we would like to ask you some questions," said Mr. Mascalco.

"Of course," she said blankly.

As she preceded the Mascalcos into the house, she

felt as if she was walking through water. It was an almost physical sensation of pressure, a buoyant feeling of absolute unreality.

While the Mascalcos sat on the couch where Catherine had huddled the night before with their son's blood on her clothes and hands, she made coffee and carried it in to them.

The couple touched her so deeply that a little of her drifting sensation ebbed away. She felt her rage dissolving at the edges as she responded to their grief, their bewilderment at the death of their oldest child and only son.

Mrs. Mascalco wept and apologized for weeping. Her husband sat with his arm around her, his face distorted with emotion.

They asked her questions.

I must be careful, she told herself repeatedly.

It would shock them, and they might well hate her, when they discovered their son had died not because he possessed information dangerous to the murderer but because he had rented a house from Catherine.

"We would like to go into the house," Mrs. Mascalco said finally. "We need to get some of his things for the funeral. One of his suits."

"No," said Catherine sharply, jolted back into complete awareness. They couldn't see the old office the way it was. She could hardly bear to think of walking through the spattered hall herself, though that was where she must go as soon as they left.

"His brown suit," Mrs. Mascalco said. "A tie."

"I want to see where my son died," said her husband.

"No," Catherine said firmly.

Tom's father, she saw, was passing from grief to anger, ready to take issue with anything.

Catherine got blanker of face and firmer of voice. She remembered what the scene of her parents' crash had looked like. She had seen the car, too.

She promised to get them the suit. No, not now, later. The sheriff had sealed the house, Catherine told them. She wondered, after she said it, if that was true.

Go, she urged them silently. Go.

But they wanted to know more details about the night before. They wanted to linger with Catherine. After all, she had been with their son when he died.

Catherine finally thought of offering them food, but she could think of nothing she had in enough quantity for three people. As if she could eat—but she would have to put up a pretense.

At last Mr. Mascalco looked at his watch.

"My God, Elise, we have to go," he said.

After many leave-takings, they departed, obviously puzzled by Catherine's increasingly tense manner. They couldn't reconcile the time and effort she had given them with the chilly, fixed blankness of her face.

"I'll get the suit tomorrow," she told them. "I'll send it up the fastest way I can."

She took their address. Reassured by her sincerity, Tom's parents were finally out the front door and into their car.

After she made sure their headlights were pointing in the right direction, toward the highway, she shut the door.

Headlights, she thought. It's dark. It's night.

She had to move, and move fast. The murderer would act tonight, too.

Perhaps the evidence had already disappeared from its hiding place. He would not have to wait very late. After all, he knew that tonight Tom really wouldn't be there.

Moving swiftly, clumsy in her urgency, she rummaged through a kitchen drawer for the extra keys to the old office. The police had Tom's, but she had a set of her own. While searching, she found her gun where she had thrust it the night before.

"Always check your gun before you use it," her father had said.

She hadn't last night, but she did now. She had re-loaded Saturday morning, before she found Leona's body. The gun was ready.

She had started out the back door when a new thought struck her. If anything happened to her—No, she said. Face it. If I am killed, no one else will know what I know.

She had left the Dr. Croft column on Randall's desk, but she hadn't told him about Betty's account of the mysterious interview in Dr. Linton's office shortly before the fatal accident. Betty's story was not essential, but it was corroborative—though Betty hadn't seen the man's face.

The only solid proof was in that file in the attic. She must at least tell someone else that it existed, and then move as fast as possible.

She went back to the telephone, and dialed the *Gazette* number. Randall answered.

"Listen," she said. Then it was too much like her call the night before. She had to wait for a wave of dizziness to pass.

"Catherine, is that you? What's wrong? Where are you?"

"I'm at home, Randall. I have to tell you some-thing. Have you read that column?"

"Yes," he said. "I'm listening."

"This is what I'm going to do," she said. "And why."

"Wait for me!" he was saying almost before she finished telling him.

"No," she replied. "I have to go now."

She hung up before he could say anything else.

The Mascalcos' departure had given her back her rage. She was across the moonlit yard, through the hedge, walking up to the back door. Carried along by her anger, she felt strong as a lion. But her body was telling her something quite different, she found as she approached the old office. She had to stop and wait for a wave of weakness to pass, before she could go on.

I should be afraid, she realized. I should be afraid.

She had to fit the rage somewhere in her tired body, shift it so it could be borne. It was threatening to dispose of her.

With difficulty she fit the key in the lock. The moonlight made her arms look eerily gilded. She thought of how clearly she could be seen if anyone was watching.

But still she was not afraid.

The back door swung open. The moon shone in on the white walls covered with dark splotches. A tiny shiver edged along her spine.

The attic door was in this hallway.

She switched on the light and looked up. There was the dangling cord. She laid her gun on the floor, so she could use both hands to reach it. But the old house was high-ceilinged, and she couldn't stretch far enough to grasp the cord.

Leona had pulled it down for her the last time she had gone up in the attic.

Catherine remembered the stool that had been in Tom's kitchen on Sunday. She went to fetch it.

At last she could reach the cord. She pulled, and the rectangular wooden slab that fit into the ceiling descended. She pulled out the flimsy stairs that lay folded against it.

The single railing was weak, and Catherine remembered worrying that it might give way while she and Leona were maneuvering the filing cabinets up those narrow folding stairs.

Almost as an afterthought, she picked up the gun. Then she ascended into blackness.

The only light in the attic was a bare bulb in the middle of the sloping roof. She yanked the string dangling from it, and the attic was flooded with light.

She had played there as a child. Then it had held trunks of her grandmother's old clothes. Now it only contained two filing cabinets, sitting close to the top of the stairs in the only area where a person could stand upright.

The slots no longer had labels, so Catherine had to go through each drawer looking for the file she wanted. There weren't many left. That helped. Few people were so healthy they hadn't needed to see a doctor at least once since her father's death.

Of course, the murderer hadn't dared to.

When she opened the second cabinet she found what she wanted in the top drawer. She saw immediately that this was the file she was looking for. It had been sealed around the edges with heavy tape. On one side of that tape, there was a slit.

Father did his best to keep Leona from finding out, Catherine thought sadly.

She slid the contents of the file through the slit that Leona Gaites had made in the tape.

She turned to the last entry on the medical record.

"Biopsy taken," her father had written. "Results: saw *Mycobacterium leprae*. Evidence of Hansen's disease."

Carl Perkins was a leper.

*

"He didn't have to do it," she whispered. She rested her head against the metal of the cabinet.

It wasn't readily infectious, Dr. Croft had pointed out, deriding medieval prejudices. It needn't result in the deformities people associated with the word *leprosy*. It could be treated very effectively now. According to Dr. Croft, researchers had found the nine-banded armadillo very useful in their tests to determine even better treatment.

Four people had died because of a man's fear of exposure—a family-proud man from Louisiana, where leprosy was endemic; a man who had established himself in the town and enjoyed its respect and admiration; a man who could not bear to see that town, and more crucially his precious, insensitive son (Josh the athlete; the baseball player) turn from him in revulsion.

Had her father ever realized how dangerous Carl Perkins was? Dr. Linton had read up on the disease—had read books on how to perform the biopsy, how to look for *Mycobacterium leprae*—all to save his old friend Carl Perkins the humiliation of going to Memphis to a doctor he didn't know. Catherine could read that in the lines of the file, and she knew her father would do that for his neighbor. But her father wouldn't have flouted the law. Cases of leprosy had to be reported to the Public Health Service.

His eyebrows, Catherine thought. That's what

happened to Mr. Perkin's eyebrows. That was why he wore long-sleeved shirts. She shuddered as she recalled glimpsing the dark macules his rolled-up sleeve had revealed. That was why he hadn't felt the scalding coffee spilled on his hand. The feeling in the hand was gone, eaten away by a little bacillus.

She recalled her walk home in the dark with him. It was then that he had found out where the files were, under the pretense of needing Josh's. Mr. Perkins had walked her home for her protection and safety, she remembered dully.

The next day, at the *Gazette*, he had checked to make sure she was not involved with Tom. Why? He would have killed Tom anyway, she thought. Maybe he would have been *sorrier* if I had said Tom was my boyfriend . . . He had just heard Tom talking to Leila there in the office. I guess he did think Tom would be out of the house; if not with me, then with Leila. Did he hear Tom make a date with Leila? No, he must not have been sure, since he tried to get me to ask Tom to have dinner with them. If I had accepted, I guess he would have made some excuse to slip out for a while . . . Then he would have come here.

Catherine roused herself and shut the filing cabinet with a definite thud that marked an end. She tucked the file under her arm and switched out the attic light.

Time to go home and wait for Randall, who would be coming. It was all over.

She would tell him everything she had thought of that afternoon while she was staring blankly at the office wall. Carl Perkins had known far in advance that he would kill her father and mother. He had already made the plane reservations to visit Josh in California, because he didn't want to go to the funeral of two people he had murdered. A strange nicety. He had been upset when he found that during his absence Lowfield had acquired a new doctor much faster than anyone could have expected. The presence of a new doctor muddled the question of where the records would be kept and who would have charge of them. And then Leona Gaites stepped in, with the damning file. Who would ever know what had tripped her memory, what had made her search those filing cabinets while Catherine was downstairs preparing the old office for Tom's rental? How long Carl Perkins had paid for her silence, until, in the frenzy of a man driven too far, he came into her home and killed her . . . and after a desperate search found that the file was not there.

Where could it be?

Why, the old Purloined Letter ruse.

It was with the other files.

Or maybe he made Leona tell him before she died, Catherine thought for the first time, as she slowly descended the attic stairs.

Catherine slowly refolded the wooden stairs. As she was about to go out the door, she remembered she had promised Tom's parents she would send them his suit.

The bedroom had been left just as it was the night before. Averting her eyes from the rumpled bed, evidence of Tom's last moments of life and Leila, she searched through the closet until she found the suit. A matching tie was conveniently looped around the hanger.

She had turned out all the lights just before she heard the noise.

She froze with the gun in one hand, the file and suit encumbering her arm.

She didn't for one minute try to deceive herself into thinking it was Randall. She knew it was Carl Perkins.

He must have seen the light in the attic, from across the street. He knew what she had been doing. She had found the file for him. He still wanted it. He had killed four people to get that file and destroy it.

And she had left the back door unlocked, so Randall could enter.

It opened slowly.

She could see his silhouette against the moonlight streaming gently through the open door. She knew that her own white face was bathed in the same light.

"I never wanted this to happen," said Carl Perkins.

Sorry. He was *sorry*. And he would kill her, in this house, where she couldn't run.

The pang of fear she had first felt when she heard the scrabbling at the door was growing. It would do her in, if she didn't act. It was already slowing her, she tried to summon up her rage, but it wouldn't come. She was swamped by the unreality of the situation. A man she had known all her life was prepared to kill her, end her existence.

She saw the long dark shape in his hand. It was Josh's baseball bat, she knew; discarded when Josh left behind him high school sports, Lowfield, and his father.

She must act now or she would *die*.

She threw Tom's suit in his face. She wheeled and ran through the dark living room. She was saved only by the stool she had left in the hall, and by her knowledge of the house. The stool tripped him up, and the suit blinded him for a second. The lock at the front door was familiar, and her fingers worked it automatically.

Then she was outside in the night. She was down the sidewalk before he came through the door.

She almost ran across the road and out into the fields, but the instinct to seek help made her turn left, round the corner, and run back toward the town. She ran between the side of her own house and the front of Carl Perkin's mansion. Would Molly Perkins protect her if she dashed up the sidewalk and slammed down the brass knocker? It was too risky to try, and her legs picked up their speed again after a brief hesitation.

Run, run, don't look back. Her breath was loud and ragged. She was lighter than Perkins; not very swift, but then he wasn't either. His arms were strong enough to wield a baseball bat, but his legs weren't used to running.

Passing her front yard, the temptation to swerve in was almost irresistible. But she had left the front door locked, and it would take too much time to open it. Run, run farther, don't get trapped.

The gun. I have a gun.

It had just been something she was clutching along with the file.

She was now under the streetlight a block past her house. She wheeled, dropped the file.

Her knees bent slightly, her head snapped back,

her left arm came up to grip her right forearm, and she fired. The sound ripped the night in two.

He kept running toward her.

He doesn't think I can hit him, she thought, with an odd cold rush of amusement.

She took careful aim and fired again.

She killed him.

For a long second she didn't understand the significance of the emptiness beyond the barrel of the gun. Then her arms fell to her sides. She straightened. For the moment of detachment she had remaining, she felt considerable pride in that shot. Her father would have been proud.

Then the detachment melted away forever, and she was Catherine Linton, shivering with cold in the oppressive heat of the summer night. The locusts were singing.

She walked toward the sprawled figure in the middle of the street. She stood over Carl Perkins's body. The file, with its contents spilled out onto the pavement, lay forgotten behind her. She felt for a pulse she knew she would not feel.

Doors were opening down the street. There were shouts of alarm.

Then there was the sound of rapid light footsteps

moving toward her. Molly Perkins was running down the street.

Catherine flinched away from the body, and took four rapid steps backward to stand under the streetlight. She turned away. She didn't want to see Miss Molly's face. She heard the sound of the woman kneeling by her husband's body.

Then she looked. Molly Perkins was gazing at the face of her dead husband. She did not look up at Catherine. There was no indication of surprise in the woman's posture; she had been waiting for her husband's death for a long time. Maybe her grief was all spent.

A car pulled up behind Catherine. She didn't move.

Running footsteps, heavier this time.

Randall held her to him fiercely.

She let out her breath in a light sigh. Her arms dangled uselessly at her sides, the gun still clutched in her right hand.

Then there were many voices, many footsteps. She kept her face buried against Randall's chest. There was a siren, and Sherriff Galton's voice. She didn't move.

Her fingers relaxed, and the gun fell to the ground,

slid across the pavement, and went into the ditch. Her arms went up, anchored around Randall's waist.

In the noise and movement that disturbed the clear hot night, they stood joined under the bleak glare of the streetlight.

The locusts sang.

A few miles outside of Lowfield, up the highway that led to Memphis, a little boy cried over his supper because his dun-colored dog had been missing for four days.